REALM JUMPER

SILVERWOOD ACADEMY
BOOK THREE

ID JOHNSON

For Cara and Glenn for always bringing Elliott back.

CONTENTS

DOUBTERS

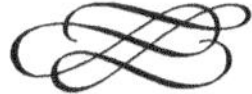

Rachael

"WHAT DID YOU SAY?" Graham asked, slowly stepping into the doorway. "What was Chell?"

Rachael swallowed. Hard. "The… vampire. There was a vampire hiding in the closet behind where Jared's standing. She ran through that window over there." Rachael pointed at the shattered glass. "I got a good look at her. I know it sounds crazy. But it was her. I'm positive."

"It must've just been someone that looked like her," Jared offered with a shrug. He set his hands on his hips. "I didn't get a good look at her. She did have the same color of hair, shape, and build… but there's no way that it could possibly have been Chell."

"I know what I saw," Rachael insisted, stepping into the dark kitchen. "Nothing is impossible at this point, is it? Maybe it's not your Chell. Maybe it's Chell from another world. All I know is what I saw. That vampire that ran through that window was Chell Knight. I'm positive."

Graham ran a hand through his hair and uttered a curse word, looking from Rachael to the broken window and then back again. "I knew we should've put a camera on you."

"Any chance Jared's camera picked her up?" Tripp asked, standing on the other side of Graham.

"We can definitely check and see. Are there any other vampires in here or was that it?" Graham asked.

"I don't see anymore." Jared checked all of the cabinets, even the tiny ones, and Rachael wasn't sure if he was being sarcastic or serious.

"All right. Let's head back," Graham suggested, and they all headed to the vehicle.

Rachael took her time, staring off into the night, wondering where the vampire had disappeared to. While she was sure it had been Chell, it didn't make any sense. Whoever it was, she was still out there and a danger to the community. Why would Chell be in that house, even if she was a vampire? Did she know the man they'd taken out, or had it been a coincidence?

On the way back to the academy, Rachael sat in the back next to Jared. He was looking at his own footage. It wasn't any help at all. While it was possible to make out the form of the woman running across the dark room to the window, it didn't show her face or any identifiable characteristics. It was even hard to tell what color her hair was, she was moving so quickly.

"This isn't going to help," Jared said, shoving his phone back into his pocket.

"Damn," Graham muttered, but it seemed to Rachael as if he didn't really mean it. She couldn't blame him for not wanting to see his fiancée in vampire form, especially after all the years they'd spent hunting and killing the undead together.

"It just doesn't make any sense," Ty said. He had no reason to go out of his way to be polite to Rachael to spare her feelings and every reason to be blunt. "If it was even possible that Chell could be a vampire, there's no reason why she'd be at that location."

"I know it doesn't make any sense," Rachael replied. "But then... nothing in my life makes sense right now."

"We can check for surveillance cameras in the area and see if there's any helpful footage," Graham said, and Rachael took that to mean that was the end of the discussion.

Rachael stared out the window for the rest of the ride, wishing she hadn't said anything at all. If it was Chell, it would've been best for someone else to make that discovery. If it wasn't, she had just upset Graham and everyone else for no reason--and she sounded crazy again. She'd sort of gotten used to sounding like a crazy person, but she didn't like it any more now than she had when she'd first taken on that characteristic.

Back at the academy, she followed the others into the building, thinking Graham would probably make an excuse as to why he couldn't stay with her that night. If it were her, Rachael would want to be alone. She'd probably want to drink herself into oblivion and look at old pictures of herself and her loved one until she passed out.

He let the others go ahead of them, waiting for her near the door, and Rachael braced herself for his excuse. Jared told them goodnight, and she waved, but then, Graham took hold of her hand. "I'm sorry I've been so quiet."

"No, it's okay. I don't blame you. I'm sorry. I shouldn't have blurted that out. I was just… shocked."

He managed a smile and brushed her hair back. "I don't know if you saw Chell or not, but I believe you believe you did. So… either that was her, or Sasha or someone else is playing tricks on you."

Rachael raised an eyebrow. She hadn't considered that was possible, but then, she'd said herself that anything was possible.

Graham put his hands around her waist and pulled her closer. "Rachael, I hope you know how much I care about you. I love you, I really do, and I want to be with you. I'm sorry everything is so screwed up right now. Being a vampire hunter means nothing is ever normal, but this is about as fucked up as I can ever remember my life being."

"You're telling me," she smirked, shaking her head.

With a chuckle, Graham let go with one hand to cup her face. "The idea that Chell might've somehow returned makes me question everything. I know she died. I know she didn't come back as a vampire. I know she's gone. It just… isn't possible. Unless she came from another world. But that's all such a mess, and none of us knows how it works. It's hard to imagine that's possible either."

"It is. Trust me." Rachael wasn't sure how alternate realities worked, but she knew she'd come from one.

He nodded. "To think she might've been living as a vampire for years in another world is something I can't allow myself to think about." A pained expression took over his face as he looked down at the ground.

"I understand." Rachael could imagine how awful that must be. She leaned up on her tiptoes and kissed his cheek. "I'm so sorry, Graham. I truly hope I was wrong."

Turning his face, he looked her in the eyes, his nose rubbing against hers. Without another word, he leaned forward and pressed his mouth to hers, and Rachael welcomed him, running her hand up to the back of his head and pulling him in tighter.

He released her lips and leaned back slightly, putting some space between them so they could both breathe. "I may be unsure about everything else in the world right now, Rachael, but I'm not unsure about you. I love you."

"I love you, too." Rachael laced her fingers around his neck and pulled him in again, smothering his mouth with hers and letting the chaos slip away, at least for the moment.

LET'S PRETEND THAT DIDN'T HAPPEN

Rachael

No one wanted to talk about what she'd seen, so Rachael decided to let it go. She still had a lot of work to do, even if she had been fully added to the team and wasn't required to do any extra training. She still went to classes with her classmates, still went to workouts on her own afterward, and still did her best to figure out what the hell was going on.

Jared kept the book she and Graham had found for weeks. Even after Rachael started asking him for it on a daily basis. She wanted it back so she could read it for herself. He'd already told her there were a few interesting tidbits in there but nothing new that he thought would help them solve any of their current problems. She didn't buy it. In the meantime, she started taking notes about the state of the world, with dates of when people mentioned certain bits of information to her. If it were possible to keep those from changing along with everything else, maybe the next time there was a shocker like there had been about Chell and Sasha's background, she'd have something notated that showed things hadn't always been that way.

The fall semester was nearly halfway over by the time Jared gave her the book back. The weather was changing, and it was turning into vampire season, a phrase Rachael had coined in her book that everyone around the academy used. She'd tried to explain that fall was the best time for them to be out and about because of their aversion to the sun and their disdain for cold weather. She'd sort of had Chell explain it to a new student at the time, and now it seemed sort of silly. But basically, this was the time of year when vampires were most active.

She'd gone on a few hunts recently, but so far nothing had happened to catch her attention since the night she'd seen Chell--or thought she'd seen Chell, anyway. The longer she went without seeing her again, the more she began thinking it was possible she really had been mistaken. Maybe whoever she'd seen just looked similar to Chell and it wasn't really her. Or maybe she was truly crazy this time. Or maybe it was Chell and everyone else was wrong.

Unless and until she saw her again, it wouldn't matter.

"I'm so jealous that you get to go on so many hunts," Jazz said one October evening as Rachael was getting ready to head out to the garage to the SUV. "We don't even get to start going on our training hunts until the spring."

"I know. I wish you could go, too," Rachael admitted. Wearing her black leather was much more comfortable now than it had been during the heat of the summer.

"Is it as fun as we all think it is?"

"Usually." Rachael sat down on the edge of her bed and pushed her feet into her boots. "The one tonight should be pretty routine. Just an old woman vampire who's been terrorizing some children."

"Like in a creepy old house?" Jazz's face lit up. Rachael recognized that feeling. She'd often felt that way before she'd been allowed to go.

"I think so. A lot of the houses we go to are pretty creepy." There'd been a few that weren't, like the house where she thought she'd seen Chell.

"Well, it's really cool that you get to go. And it's really cool that you can explode vampires' heads, too."

Rachael smiled at her, standing and making sure the holster around her waist was secured. "You'll be out there before you know it."

"Maybe." Jazz shrugged. She looked so dejected, Rachael couldn't help but feel bad for her.

A knock on her door brought her out of her head before she could say more to Jazz about getting her day. She headed over to open it and was surprised to see Jared standing there with her dad's book in his hands. "Hi. I wanted to give you this before we leave. I don't think there are any answers in there, but maybe you'll see something I didn't."

"That's really disappointing," she said, taking it from him. "With all of the promise of answering questions, doesn't there have to be something?"

He shrugged. "It's all cryptic, like my grandfather's book. But… like I said, maybe something will stand out to you that I missed."

Jazz was at the door now. "What is it?"

"Oh, shit. I didn't know you weren't alone." Jared ran a hand through his hair.

"It's okay," Rachael said with a shrug. "Here." She handed the book to Jazz. "You wanna help? See if any of this makes sense."

Jazz knew next to nothing about the situation Rachael had gotten herself into by causing the two worlds to collide--or whatever it was she'd done. But she was smart. Jared was protesting as Jazz took the book and headed to the couch, reading the title aloud and then looking questioningly at Rachael.

"Just don't take it out of this room, and don't let anyone else see it, not even Rex, okay?" Rachael hoped that would go far enough to make Jared stop stammering.

"Okay," Jazz said, her forehead crinkled with interest as she looked through the first few pages.

"You ready to go?" Rachael asked Jared.

He nodded, and she said goodbye to Jazz before they walked out. "Are you sure about that?" Jared asked her. "She doesn't really need to know about… all that."

"It'll be fine," Rachael assured him. She knew Jazz well enough by now to understand that she could be trusted. "Besides, maybe not knowing anything will help her understand better than we can."

"I guess," he said, but she could tell he was still feeling cross about the whole thing.

Rachael patted him on the arm and headed down the stairs. "What could possibly go wrong?" she asked with an exaggerated shrug, fully knowing she sounded like she was in a sitcom.

"What indeed," Jared replied, shaking his head.

Rachael laughed, but she prayed he wasn't right. Surely, giving the book to Jazz couldn't cause problems could it? With any luck, she'd be the one to figure out what had happened so they could finally understand how to fix it.

A FOG

Rachael

JAZZ HAD ASKED if it was a haunted house, and by the looks of it, the place certainly could've been. Unlike some of the other dilapidated structures Rachael had hunted in recently, this one wasn't falling over. It was just built in a gothic revival style, which made it look sinister even without a streak of lightning across the background.

"You okay?" Graham asked, resting his hand on her arm.

"Never better." She blew out a hot breath and proceeded up the walkway to the front porch.

She'd be going in the front with Graham. It had become routine in the last few months. In this case, it should be simple enough. They were only after one vampire after all. Not that there hadn't been more than a few cases where they were expecting one bloodsucker and had gotten several more.

"The forest behind the house is pretty thick," Jared said in their ears. "It backs up to a greenbelt. We'd better be careful not to lose him in there."

"Got it," Graham answered for all of them. Rachael doubted that would be a problem. This would be over so quickly, it was practically over now before it even started.

Graham opened the front door and went in first, like he always did, in an attempt to protect her should there be any vampires waiting for them. There wasn't--just a wide staircase and a dark parlor.

"Movement toward the back of the house!" Ty said frantically in their ears.

"Coming my way?" Jared asked about two seconds before the soft sound of gunfire through the silencers from the back of the house let them know the answer before anyone could speak.

"Did you get him?" Graham asked as he flew through the house to the back, Rachael on his tail.

"Nope." Jared's voice was weak over the radio, and Rachael picked up speed, afraid that meant he was injured.

They found him lying on his back on the kitchen floor, his arm spraying blood all over the walls.

"Oh, my God!" Rachael said, moving to his side. Graham produced a tourniquet he'd been carrying just in case, as this was not his first experience with someone spraying blood.

"Marcy, get down here and see if you can help Jared," Graham said as he twisted the tourniquet into place. Marcy likely had some medication that would help him.

"Our vamp is disappearing into the woods," she said, her voice echoing down the hall as she came closer.

"I'm on him," Tripp answered through the earpiece.

Rachael was torn between giving chase with Tripp and staying there with Jared. She knew Graham was leaving or else he wouldn't have called for Marcy.

"You okay?" Graham asked Jared.

"Never better." Jared rolled his eyes and sank back onto the floor. Rachael laughed despite the circumstances since she'd just had the exact same conversation with Graham herself.

"I'm going," Graham said to her. Rachael nodded. She wasn't.

"Be careful," Macy advised him as she gave some sort of liquid out of a flask to Jared. It should help with the pain, Rachael thought, maybe even start healing up any broken blood vessels. It was hard to tell in the dim light, but it didn't seem as if it was too deep of a wound. It certainly helped that Jared was wearing leather.

"You should go, Rach," Jared said as she crouched down next to him.

"I think they can handle it." She glanced out the back door, which was still open, and saw four forms moving quickly toward the trees.

"You can handle it better. He caught me off-guard," he explained. "He's fast."

"I'm sure the four of them will be all right." Rachael did have a bad feeling about this one, though, and it didn't revolve around the vampire who'd torn out of the house either. She felt as if this guy was just the bait, and whatever he was taking them to was the real problem.

"What the hell is that?" she heard Tripp say over her earpiece.

"These fucking blue lights are everywhere," Sammi said. "Has anyone ever seen anything like this before?"

Rachael looked out the back door and slowly stood up as the discussion continued. She wasn't listening, though. She was looking at a forest slowly filling up with glowing blue lights, like a thousand wisps had just arrived in the outskirts of Baltimore. It was both beautiful and terrifying at the same time.

"What in the world?" Marcy muttered, now standing over her shoulder.

"I don't know," Rachael admitted. "But I don't like it."

"Go, Rach," Jared insisted. She turned to look at him. He was getting more color back in his face, and he was able to sit up now, too.

"Are you sure?" she asked, looking at him over her shoulder, as if her mind was already made up.

"Yeah, go."

"I'll stay with him," Marcy offered, placing her hand on Rachael's shoulder in support.

With a deep breath and a nod, Rachael started walking--out the door, down the steps, across the yard, to the edge of a forest quickly filling with white fog, blue lights, and potentially deadly bloodsuckers, the likes of which she'd never seen.

LOST

Rachael

A THICK FOG rolled between the trees as Rachael approached the outskirts of the woods. When the mist touched her skin, she instantly recoiled. It was cold, wet, almost as if it was made of ice but moved like a cloud. Her teammates were in there, so not stepping through wasn't an option.

Ignoring the temperature and the fact that she was rapidly beginning to get the chills, Rachael continued to walk. The trees looked unfriendly--scraggly, with thin twigs and branches that seemed to reach for her like fingers. The bark on every tree was dark, with patches of gray that almost seemed to ooze from the gnarled, twisted trunks. Something told Rachael if she'd seen these trees a few hours earlier, during the daylight, she would've seen something far different than what she was witnessing now.

The blue lights continued to twinkle in the distance, multiplying, moving about. From here, they didn't look like wisps, though. Like electric pulses, lights floating around a disco dance floor, the blue flickers lit up the woods before her. The further she walked, the deeper the forest seemed to become.

Perhaps most troubling of all, she couldn't see or hear any of her teammates. "Graham?" she whispered, praying he would pick it up on his earpiece. "Can you hear me?"

All was still and silent.

Rachael continued on, her pace slow, her weapon before her. How was she supposed to catch up to a vampire while she was wading through a storm of fog and trees that were attempting to rip her hair out and scratch her face?

She soldiered on, listening intently for anyone or anything. She couldn't even hear Jared or Marcy anymore, which truly worried her. She tried calling their names and heard nothing.

Ahead of her, the blue lights seemed to stop moving away. It seemed like she'd reach them soon enough if she kept walking at the same pace she was currently traveling. She made another attempt to reach her teammates. "Graham? Tripp? Can you hear me?"

Nothing.

The lights were larger than she thought, but when she was within an arm's reach of them, she was hesitant to put her hand out and touch one for fear it would either burn or electrocute her. But she had to satisfy her curiosity.

Carefully, Rachael reached with one finger and tapped one of the lights. Her finger went right through, as if there was nothing there. Perhaps there wasn't. She looked behind her to see if she could figure out where they were originating from, but it was impossible to tell.

She also noted she couldn't see the house anymore either. There appeared to be nothing behind her but trees and nothing in front of her except the blue lights and more forest.

"Okay. I give up. Who's out here? What do you want?"

She didn't expect an answer. She might've been better off if one hadn't come. When she heard a voice from between the trees, she jumped. "Those are not easy questions to answer."

The voice was male, possibly middle-aged, but she couldn't see a person yet. She squinted in the direction from which it had come, but in the fog and the dim light, save the blue sparkles, she got nowhere. "Who's there?" She didn't think it was a teammate. Perhaps it was the vampire. She considered putting her gun away so she could ready her hands to do some exploding.

"You don't know?" he asked. "That's disappointing."

She saw him then, stepping between the trees, maybe half a football field away. "Why would I know who you are?"

"I certainly know who you are, Rachael. It's been too long, but I know exactly who you are. It's too bad you have yet to figure out exactly who you are for yourself."

His words were puzzling, almost like a riddle. He continued to walk closer. "Are you making these lights?"

"No."

"Who is?"

"You are."

"I am?" Rachael almost laughed. "No, I'm definitely not making them."

"Oh, but you are, Rachael."

She shook her head. "And I suppose I'm making the fog, too?"

"Not exactly. That always happens when one calls the lights."

"I didn't call the lights. Where's my team?"

"Here and there."

"Are they all right?"

"Can't say."

"Did you harm any of them?" He was about fifteen feet away now.

"No, I didn't. I hope nothing did. But I haven't seen them."

"Then how do you know they're here and there?"

"Oh, Rachael. You've always asked so many questions. It's so good to see you again."

Then, she realized who she was talking to. His was a face she hadn't seen in so long, it was like a memory drudged from the depth of the seas. Yet, he looked exactly the same as she remembered. "How did you…?"

He didn't answer her, only spread his arms wide and wrapped them around her. "It's so good to finally see you… my daughter."

DEAREST DAD

Rachael

THE SOUND of those words leaving the mouth of a stranger had Rachael holding her breath. She'd known who he was the moment he stepped through the fog, but to be face to face with him now, her father, the man she'd assumed had walked out on her and her mother all those years ago, was overwhelming. "Where have you been?" she asked, trying to keep her tone even. There was no point in accusing him of anything when there was a possibility he'd been gone this whole time for reasons he could not control.

"It doesn't matter where I've been. It only matters where you've been. Where you are. Where you're going."

"It does matter where you've been," she disagreed. "We thought you left us. Mom had no idea where you were off to. She assumed you'd just decided you didn't want to have anything to do with us anymore. Were you stuck in another realm?"

"I was. But now I'm free. Thanks to you."

"Me?" Rachael couldn't believe that was true. "I haven't done anything to try to free you."

"You've done a lot, Rachael. Most of it, you don't even realize you've done. That's part of the problem, though. You're going to have to stop casting that magic of yours around all over the place. It's going to get you into trouble."

Rachael ran her hand through her hair trying to figure out what he was getting at. "So I freed you? Did I change Sasha and Chell's background, too? Did I somehow make Chell a vampire?"

Billy took a deep breath and let it out slowly, and Rachael felt herself calming down as well, as if he'd cast a spell over her. The fog was still thick, but it didn't come between them. The lights continued to twinkle, but kept their distance as well, as if nothing should interrupt this quality time between a man and his daughter who hadn't seen each other for years.

"I can answer all of those specific questions, but it will take some time, something I do not presently have. Rachael, you and I are scribes. We have the ability to hear and record tales from other realms and weave them into stories. This can be problematic, as you have discovered, when we take what we think is fiction and destroy actual lives with our words."

"So I did kill Chell," Rachael muttered.

"No. You described what happened to Chell--in one realm, in one possible reality of thousands. Then, when that reality was not to your liking, you summoned more realities. One of them is where we are trapped here now, as I was once trapped in another world through the words of another scribe. What you need to know, Rachael, is that there should be limitations on your writing. Never, ever write yourself into a story again. This is how worlds collide. Also, bear in mind it is easier to record without changing if a hundred years or more have passed."

"You mean I shouldn't write about anyone who's still alive?"

"Precisely."

"But how would I know that when I thought I'd created everyone I was writing about?"

"It is best to use the caution of historical accounts, dear."

Rachael nodded--he was telling her not to write anything contemporary at all. "Is there any way I can fix what's happened to Chell?"

"No. You didn't do that."

She blew out a hot breath of frustration. While it was reassuring to know that she hadn't been responsible for Chell's death, she'd hope she could fix it. "What about this vampire version of her? Can I help her?"

"Alas, no. Whether in this world or her old one, she must be destroyed as all vampires must be."

"So… everything that's been done cannot be changed. This world is destined to be full of vampires now."

"When two worlds collide, there is some of the old from each. They create a new world. Fragments of the two will combine and make a new reality. You cannot change what's been done, but you can safeguard this world from any other collisions."

Rachael's eyebrows arched. "How?"

Billy let out a sigh. "It is in the book. I'm afraid I cannot tell you more at the moment. I must go."

"Go? But, you just got here."

"I know that, Rachael, but this is not my world. It never was. Now that you've brought two new realities together, I cannot stay here for long. As you see, the power from which I've come grows weak."

Rachael noticed the lights were not nearly as bright as they had been a few moments ago. "Where are you headed?" she asked, wishing there was a way he could stay.

"I must continue on my quest, to find the origin of vampires and eliminate that origin. My duties take me elsewhere for now, but never doubt the strength and power that runs through your veins, Rachael. The Barnes family has always been powerful, since the dawn of our existence in a realm where magic is strong and vampires quake at the mention of our name. I will attempt to come back to you one day. Just remember my warning about your writing. Stay here, continue to fight evil, and you may well rid this realm of the dangers of night stalkers."

The fog rolled in between them again, and Billy began to back away. "But wait...." She could hardly see him through the thick clouds of gray. "Dad--wait!"

Rachael hurried forward, hoping she could catch him before he disappeared for good. There were so many things she wanted to say to him, so many things she needed to know.

Unable to see, she staggered forward, tripping and falling forward. Her hands broke the fall, but her knee caught a gnarled root, and it gashed into her flesh. The pain was a stinging sensation that lingered even as she attempted to pull herself up. With her vision obscured, she didn't realize how close she was to the trunk of a tree until her head rammed into it. Still calling for her dad, she closed her eyes, and the fog-covered forest rolled away.

FOUND

Rachael

"Rachael! Open your eyes!"

The sound of Graham's voice, and his strong hands on her shoulders, had her coming around--eventually. Rachael slitted her eyes and saw the sun was up. Her head was aching, and she tasted blood in her mouth.

As soon as she saw him, everything came back to her, and she scrambled up to sitting, going too fast and giving herself an even worse headache. "Easy... easy..." he said, his hands never leaving her. "Are you all right?"

Rachael looked around. She was still sitting in the forest, but the sun was up enough that it was no longer dark. The fog was gone, as were the blue lights. She could see the tops of a few houses in the distance, though, and she remembered thinking she couldn't see any houses at all before, when it had been dark and foggy. "I'm okay."

"Yeah? God, you scared the hell out of us." Graham sat back on one heel, his other knee bent in front of him. "We've been looking for you for hours."

"How is that possible?" she asked. "The woods around here aren't that deep."

"I know. And I swear I looked here a dozen times, but I couldn't find you." He brushed the hair back from her eyes and said something into his earpiece about meeting them at the SUV soon.

"How's Jared?" she asked, suddenly remembering he'd been injured.

"He's fine. I had Miguel come and get him a few hours ago, though. Sitting on the kitchen floor of a rundown house wasn't doing him any favors. Could you not hear us on the radio?"

"No. Could you hear me? As soon as that fog rolled out, it was like I lost contact with everyone."

"I could hear everyone but you," he said, shaking his head. "What happened? How did you hit your head?"

Her hand immediately went to the spot on her forehead. She could feel a knot, and it was caked with blood. "I hit my head in the fog," she said, remembering chasing after her dad before she'd fallen. Her pants were torn at the knee, too. She must've fallen hard because it was difficult to rip leather. "Did you get the vampire?"

Again, Graham was shaking his head. "We lost him in the fog."

"I'm not surprised."

"We still don't know where it came from."

The words of her father came back to her. "I made it," she said. Graham turned and looked at her, both eyebrows raised as if to ask why. "Not on purpose. My dad... my dad said I'd done it. I opened something."

"Wait--what? Your dad? You saw your dad?" His eyes were bulging out of his head, and she couldn't blame him for thinking she was delusional, but she could remember the conversation and knew it was real. She likely had it on video, too, since she was also wearing a camera. But then... if it had been working, why had it taken so long for Graham to find her? He should've had her coordinates.

"Rachael?" He had his hand on her leg. "Did you hear me? I asked what he said."

"Oh... he said a lot of stuff. Mostly, he tried to explain how the collisions work, how a new world is basically formed from the old two, and that I should only write about people that have to be dead. And never myself."

"So… he confirmed your writing did this?"

She nodded. "I caused the two worlds to collide. But he said I didn't actually kill Chell. That was just me reporting, not something I did. He said an infinite number of worlds exist, and I did bring a different version of Chell here when I was trying to bring her back. He said I summoned the changed history between Chell and Sasha as well, that it came from another realm."

Graham's eyebrows knit together. "So you can change some of our memories and what we've done through your writing by causing more realities to collide?"

She shrugged. "He said it's all in the book, and he didn't have time to answer all of my questions right now, but that the book would, and that he had to go. He did say he had been stuck in another realm at one point, though. That's where he was, so it wasn't as if he meant to abandon me and my mother." The realization that her own reality had essentially changed set in. Her father hadn't decided he didn't want her. He'd just been trapped in another realm.

"It sounds like we've gotten a few answers, but just as many questions," Graham said, running his hand through his hair. "I say, we go back to the academy, get you cleaned up, sleep on it, and then think about it later."

Rachael nodded. "Maybe Jazz found some information in the book."

"You gave her the book?"

"Yeah. She wanted to help, and even though Jared didn't seem to think it would be of any use to her, we decided to let her have it for a while. Why?"

"No reason. She just doesn't have all the background information. And… I hope no one else takes an interest in it."

The idea that someone--namely Sasha--would want it did come to mind. Suddenly, Rachael was in a huge hurry to get back to Jazz. Surely, if something had happened to her, someone would've contacted Graham by now. "We should hurry," Rachael noted.

Graham took her hand, and they hurried off to the SUV. The fact that Rachael had to have been somewhere else, other than the forest, in order for Graham not to see her, was in the back of her mind, but she didn't have time to question where she might've been at the moment. She needed to make sure everything at home was as it should be.

BOOKED

Rachael

WHEN THEY GOT BACK to the academy, Jazz was asleep in her room. The fan was roaring as usual, but Graham managed to unlock the door so they could see the girl with their own eyes, and Rachael even checked that she was breathing. Then, they went back to her room and made sure the book was still there, which it was.

"Feel better?" Graham asked as Rachael picked up the book and flipped through it.

"I do. But I don't understand why Jared said he thinks the book won't help us with any of our issues, but my dad said that it had all of the answers."

"I don't know. Maybe because it was written by someone with your skills, it will only make sense to someone with your skills." Graham shrugged and sank down next to her on the couch.

"Maybe so." Rachael didn't feel like reading it right now. Her head was pounding, and she knew she needed a shower. And a nap. She'd worry about the book later.

Setting it down on the coffee table, she turned to Graham. "Where do you think I was all that time? It doesn't make sense that you couldn't find me in the woods. Do you think I might've been in another realm?"

He raised his eyebrows. "I don't know. But I'd like to think we just missed you."

"I couldn't hear you, and you couldn't hear me."

"Maybe there was something wrong with your earpiece."

"I guess." She didn't think that was the case, though. "I'm going to go take a shower. Care to join me?"

Graham smiled at her. "I thought you'd never ask." He leaned down and kissed her, and all thoughts of the book, vampires, and everything else, went out of her head.

With her head injury, Graham was careful with her. He took her into the shower and helped her undress while the water heated up. Then, he took his own clothing off and followed her beneath the heated flow.

He took his time washing her hair and cleaning the dried blood from her forehead. It was nice to have his hand lathering her hair up and sliding over her body with the soap suds.

When she was all clean, she helped Graham wash his back.

All of their careful cleaning was for nothing a moment later when he began to kiss her deeply, and Rachael found herself melting in his arms. When he lifted her and pressed her against the shower wall, she gladly wrapped her legs around him.

The feel of him sliding inside of her had a soft moan leaving her lips. He felt so good, even though she was exhausted, and her muscles were sore. Slowly, he thrust in and out of her, his mouth working over her neck and earlobes as Rachael kept her eyes closed and breathed him in, concentrating on the feel of him.

If they hadn't been in a dormitory with huge hot water heaters, they likely would've ran out of warm water by the time Graham finally thrust into her one last time and filled her with his warm essence.

Rachael unwrapped her legs, and when her feet were settled on the shower floor again, Graham lathered up her sponge and carefully washed between her legs. The feel of the material against her clit had her legs quaking again.

Graham chuckled. "You ready to go again?"

"Not now," she told him. "Too tired."

"I hope you don't have a concussion."

She opened her eyes to see him staring at her head wound.

"I'm fine," she assured him, and helped clean him up again, still reveling in the feel of him.

Later, after Graham had gone home, Rachael sat on the bed and stared at the book. When she opened it, the table of contents suddenly seemed more alive than it had that day in the library, and she quickly thumbed to the section she needed, as if something within her was guiding her now.

"How to kill vampires from other realms," she read. That was something she'd need to read in order to get rid of the new Chell she'd accidentally summoned. It was similar to killing the vampires they were used to, except for the fact that she'd have to open a portal between the two worlds in order to prevent the vampire from reappearing in the other world. "Open a portal? Seems easy enough." Rachael rolled her eyes.

The details of how to do that were pretty well written. Her father had explained it in great detail and included the magical words she'd need to say and how to pronounce them. She'd be calling on a magic deep within her as a hunter and a writer. She was likely the only one on her team who'd be able to defeat the new Chell vampire.

"So what about Sasha?" she asked aloud, hoping whatever had led her to this section of the book would respond again.

But then she realized it wouldn't have to. "That's not our Sasha!" she proclaimed. "That's a Sasha from another realm. Our Sasha is still captured by Chell's spell. It didn't break when she died. I just somehow managed to summon her from another realm as well. So… in order to defeat her, I'll have to use the same spell that I'll use to defeat Chell."

It all sounded easy enough--but saying it was a lot different than actually doing it. She leaned her head back on her pillow and stared at the ceiling. Talking to her dad had helped, even though she had no idea why it had helped. As long as she had this book, she felt like she could manage just about anything that came along.

"Hey, girl! You decent?" Jazz's voice called from the hallway. She didn't wait to crack open the door.

Sitting up, Rachael called, "Hi! Yeah, come on in."

Jazz came and sat on the end of the bed. "How did it go last night?"

Not knowing where to begin, Rachael let out a sigh. "It was crazy. But we all made it back, and that's what counts."

"Yeah, I heard Doc got his arm scratched. Is he okay?"

Realizing she hadn't even bothered to check on Jared, she said, "I hope so."

"Looks like you got a cut yourself. Your head all right?"

Rachael raised a hand to the sore spot in the middle of her forehead. "I'll live. Things got really weird last night. I don't even know how to describe all of it."

Jazz lifted an eyebrow. "Crazy how?"

"Like… my dad showed up and talked to me for a few minutes. He stepped out of a portal in the middle of a foggy woods full of blue lights. Yeah, it was weird."

The girl stared at her for a minute. "Well, I thought I was gonna lose your book for a while last night."

"Why is that?" Rachael asked, her blood running cold.

"I heard that tapping sound you heard that night on the window, the night you swore Sasha was trying to break in here."

"She did break in here. You heard that sound?"

"Yep."

Rachael's eyes were bulging. "Did she come in again?"

"Nope. There's a spell in that book that binds all vampires from touching it, but it only lasts for twenty-four hours at a time. I cast the spell, and the tapping stopped. I figured they decided not to bother as long as that spell was on it."

"You're shitting me! Where?"

Jazz opened the book, flipped a few pages, and showed Rachael. "Right here. You can cast it again, but any one person can only cast it one time."

Rachael looked it over. "That's crazy. Things just keep getting weirder and weirder."

"Yeah, I bet they weren't counting on me being able to cast it and that whole hunt was to draw you away so they could grab the book."

"But how did they even know you had it?"

"I'm not sure, but I think it has some sort of magical signal that radiates out of it, like they can follow it, or something. I don't think it's a beacon intended for that, but I bet they can feel it in the universe. There's a whole chapter about vibrations from people and objects. If you can tune into the specific vibrations of a person or an item, you can follow it."

Rachael knew she'd have to study that chapter closely. Maybe she could use it to find Sasha or Chell. "I'll read it. What time does the spell wear off?"

"Three fifteen in the morning. Hey, maybe you could use it to lure her out into the open."

"Good idea. Maybe I could use it to lure her out into the open and let her take it from me, or kill all of us."

Jazz laughed. "That's not exactly what I had in mind."

"Then you don't know me very well." Rachael didn't know if she would be able to learn how to get rid of Sasha and Chell before 3:00 that morning.

"It was just a suggestion. Okay--I gotta go. There's a cute boy waiting for me in the gym. We're gonna shoot some hoops. You wanna come?"

"Do you want me to come?"

"Not even a little bit."

Rachael laughed. "Good because I've got a book to study. And should probably sleep. Eventually." She watched Jazz leave and couldn't help but smile at her. Even with everything going on in the world, that girl was still boy crazy.

Turning to the chapter about vibrations, she said, "Okay, Daddy, talk to me," and started reading, hoping she could find the answers she needed to end this thing with Sasha once and for all.

DRAW HER OUT

Rachael

RACHAEL WAS RELIEVED to see that Jared had recovered from his wounds. He still had a bandage around his arm, but he refused to use a sling, and even though she could see him wince every once in a while, he seemed to be okay. He was sitting on the couch in his living room, Graham and Rachael in chairs across from him sorting through the situation.

After she carefully studied the chapter about the vibrations in the book, she thought she had a decent handle on what she needed to do.

"You think you can draw Sasha out into the open through reading her vibrations?" Jared asked, his forehead furrowed as he studied her face.

Graham sighed on her behalf. "It sounds crazy, but then, so do vampires to most people."

"What have we got to lose?" Rachael asked him.

Jared shrugged and ran his hands through his hair. "Nothing. Except for teammates' lives."

"But that's a possibility any time we go out there. We know that when we sign up for this job, right?" Rachael reminded him.

"Yes, that's true. Ordinarily, I wouldn't have an issue with it, Rachael. I'm just worried… about you."

"Me?" she repeated. "Why is that?"

"Because for some reason Sasha wants you. She seems to think you turned her into a vampire."

"I think she's angry that I brought her here. I'm almost certain this Sasha is not the same one you hunted for all of those years. I think she's still trapped in the cave where Chell sealed her up. This Sasha is from a different world, like me. When I was trying to change things, I ended up summoning her here, and now she's trapped. I could try to send her back to where she came from, but there's no point in that when I can kill her here."

"Unless you can't kill her," he said, with the sort of shrug one gives when they are trying to be honest but don't want to hurt someone's feelings.

"Listen, Jared, I know it's nerve-wracking having Rachael in that type of danger when she's so new to the profession, but we need to utilize her powers, we both know she's more capable of ending Sasha than any of the rest of us. She might not be able to take her out all by herself, but with the rest of us there, I hope she'll be able to end her once and for all. I just need you to agree so we can get the rest of the team on board. And… I wanted to make sure you're feeling up to it."

"Feeling up to it?" Jared echoed. "Of course, I'm feeling up to it. My arm's fine. It's just a flesh wound."

Rachael laughed at his quote of a popular cult movie, but she didn't think the rest of what Jared had to say was funny. "We'll get a good plan together, make sure we are all on the same page. Then, we'll see if we can lure her out."

"And, just in case she does end up taking the book, we'll photograph every page of it first so at least we'll have a copy."

"What if her having the book is detrimental for other ways, though? Is there anything in that book that can help her overpower us?"

"Didn't you read it?" Rachael asked him. "Did you see anything in there that could be detrimental?"

"I didn't see anything, but a lot of the book didn't make much sense to me. It was like it was written in another language."

Rachael raised an eyebrow at him. She hadn't had the same experience at all. "What are you talking about?" She had the book in a bag next to her chair. Pulling it out, she handed it over to him. "Show me."

Jared took the book, his expression showing he wasn't enthusiastic about it. Swallowing hard, he opened it up and began to flip through.

Almost immediately, a puzzled expression came over his face. "Rachael, this book isn't the same as it was the last time I saw it."

"What? What do you mean?" She leaned forward to see the book, even though it was upside down.

"I mean… you know how we've been talking about things changing? This book has been rewritten since I handed it over to you yesterday. Before, much of it was written in random words that didn't even form complete thoughts. Now, it's sorted itself out and it makes sense."

"Are you sure you're not the one who's been sorted out?" Graham asked, and Rachael agreed with him, even if he was just being silly, though she didn't think that was the case.

Jared narrowed his eyes. "Yes, I'm sure. Maybe when your dad came through the portal, he straightened it out."

"Then maybe you should read it again," Rachael said.

"Before we go out tonight? I don't think I'll have time for that."

"Can you take an hour or so and look through it, make sure there's nothing in there that will help Sasha?"

"I can, but I'm not sure it matters. If the book can change, who's to say that it won't say something else to her when it's in her hands? My recommendation would be to make sure she doesn't get her hands on it."

He was right, Rachael realized that. "All right, but we can't leave it at the academy either. If it has a vibration that calls to Sasha, as Jazz mentioned, we need it to be with us."

"Do you think it just acquired that quality when your dad came through the portal last night?" Jared asked.

It was Rachael's turn to shrug. "I have no idea. Maybe so. Sasha had never been interested in it before. It was like that spell Jazz cast came into existence just when she needed it."

"Potentially from your father. Maybe he is aware of what's going on and can help us with things like that, even when he's not here," Graham suggested.

"Maybe so. I hope that's the case because we're going to need his help, and everyone else's, in order to get rid of Sasha once and for all."

"So tonight's the night, and there's nothing I can say to talk you out of it?" Jared asked.

Rachael nodded. "Tonight's the night."

Jared sighed. "Okay, then. I sure hope this works."

"You and me both," Rachael agreed. She looked at Graham, and he gave her a reassuring smile, but inside, she felt like dragons were battling. This wouldn't be easy, but she was ready to take Sasha Thornsby down once and for all.

WILL IT WORK?

Rachael

A THOUSAND STARS shone down from overhead as Rachael stood in an open field east of town. The green grass was vivid in the moonlight, waving in a gentle breeze that would've seemed calm and peaceful under any other circumstances.

Rachael was standing in the middle of the meadow alone, seeking to draw out a killer.

Her team was nearby. Woods dotted the area to her left and right, as well as directly behind her. The space in front of her was wider, but since she had no idea which direction Sasha might come from, it was hard to say where she should look, so she kept an eye out in every direction.

Her teammates weren't just behind and between the trees; they were in the tops of them, helping her keep a look out for Sasha. She was nervous that her earpiece might go out again, but if that was the case, she had a signal she was to make so that Graham could see and come to her aid. That is... as long as no thick fog rolled in. If that happened again, she would potentially be on her own.

There was no reason to think that Sasha could summon fog, though. Rachael assumed that her father had done that the night before, as well as the flashing blue lights, even though he said she'd done it herself. That made no sense. She expected Sasha to either send out a group of her minions or show up to face her alongside them. But Rachael knew she wouldn't come alone. And she knew she wouldn't trust Rachael to be alone either.

After hours of discussion, the team had finally agreed to do this, but they also had determined it was best to bring everyone they had available. That included several students. Anyone who'd been on at least two observations was also there amongst the veterans. Graham had called some nearby teams as well. Rachael should've felt at ease knowing there were over thirty hunters there to back her up. But she had no idea how any of that would measure up against Sasha.

At first, she'd stood there in the meadow, the book in one hand, her face set in defiance as she called out to the universe to send its worst. As time wore on and no vampires came by, Rachael began to doubt Jazz's theory that the book could do anything. The time her neighbor had declared would allow the book to be able to send out vibrations to Sasha again had come and gone, and Rachael was getting a little tired of waiting.

Even with her sending out her own vibrations, or trying to, nothing was happening--except Rachael was starting to get a headache.

"How much longer are we going to stay up here?" Sammi asked around the same time that Rachael was about to give up herself.

"We've only been here a little over an hour," Graham replied. "Let's give it some time."

"I thought we were under the impression she wanted this book so badly she'd show up immediately to snatch it out of Barnes's hands the second she stepped foot out into the meadow," Sammi continued, undeterred by Graham's assessment.

"We had no idea what was going to happen," the leader insisted. "All we know is, she either wants the book or Rachael or both. So... here we are."

"And she's supposed to have some sort of homing device that brings her to the middle of this field in Pennsylvania, even though the last time anyone saw her, it was in Baltimore?" Sammi wasn't letting up.

"Did you have something better to do with your time tonight, Sam?" Tripp asked. Rachael was glad she wasn't having to argue with Sammi herself.

"Not particularly, but anything would be better than this shit. I'm getting down."

"Sammi, stay put," Graham said.

"My fucking leg is asleep!"

"Sammi!"

It was impossible for Rachael to know what happened next because she couldn't actually see Sammi, but the trainer seemed to be heading down the tree from what she could gather from the noise on her earpiece.

She heard Graham swear under his breath and wondered if he realized it was loud enough for everyone to pick up, or if he'd even care if he knew that it was. Then, everyone seemed to be quiet, as if they were listening to see if Sammi was making her way back up the tree.

The silence was deafening as Rachael strained to hear what was happening. Since she couldn't see anyone else, it was also worrisome. For a few moments, she thought maybe she'd lost contact with everyone, but then Marcy asked, "Sammi where are you?"

There was no answer, so Marcy repeated the question, and Miguel asked as well. Still, Sammi said nothing.

"Does anyone see Sammi?" Jared asked.

"No," a few people said at once.

"Sammi, wherever you are, you'd better get the hell back over here now," Graham said, his tone even but the urgency evident with each word.

"Sammi?" he questioned. Still nothing. "Son of a bitch. Where the hell did she go?"

"Do you want me to go after her?" Tripp asked.

"No. I told her not to go. Just give her a few minutes," Graham replied.

"Graham, she might be in trouble," Jared reminded him calmly.

"Then maybe she'll learn her lesson," the leader said matter-of-factly.

"Graham…." Jared didn't get to finish that sentence. Before he could say more, a blood curdling scream filled the night air.

"Was that Sammi?" Rachael asked, once the noise dissipated.

"I sure the hell hope not," Graham said. "Anything that could make Sammi Knight scream like that has to be very, very bad."

SAMMI'S GONE

Rachael

THE SOUND of Sammi's screams made the hairs stand up on the back of Rachael's neck. Never in her life could she remember hearing a sound quite like that. It was as if a puppy had gotten hit by a Zamboni machine and was slowly being smooshed to death--screeching all the while.

Tripp was out of the tree and headed to the sound's origin before anyone else could physically react. "Hold up now," Graham said as others started heading out of their trees. "We can't all go running off."

"Who do you want to stay and who do you want to go?" Miguel asked.

Quickly, Graham organized a team to go check on Sammi while the others held the perimeter around Rachael's location. She found herself holding her breath waiting to find out what was the matter with Sammi.

But word didn't come--not right away anyhow. It was almost as if the second the teammates who'd gone to help exited the trees, they went radio silent. "What's going on?" Graham asked after several of his radio calls for updates seemed to fall on deaf ears. "Is anyone hearing me?"

"I don't like this," Marcy said from her position in the trees to Rachael's left. "I don't like it at all."

It was bizarre to think that none of their teammates could hear them. For all Rachael knew, a battle was raging in the woods not so far away, and she was standing there like a dumbass holding a book.

A few of the other teammates who'd stayed behind tried calling but didn't get an answer either. "We should go check on them," Jared suggested. "All of us."

"You mean call this off?" Graham asked.

It sounded like a good idea to Rachael. Clearly, she'd been wrong about the book's power to summon Sasha, and she'd also been wrong to think she could mentally call the vampire out into the open. She was just about to agree with Jared when a cold chill went up her spine, and once again she found the hairs on her neck standing on end.

Something was behind her. She felt it before she even turned her head. The hunters in the trees to her rear either hadn't noticed, or none of them were left, but Rachael knew the second she turned her head, she'd see Sasha standing there. Whether or not she'd be alone was yet unknown, but she was about to find out.

With a deep breath, Rachael turned around.

About twenty feet away, Sasha hovered over the green grass, the tips of her boots dragging along the tops of the plants as she fluttered in like an ethereal, demonic butterfly. Rachael took a deep breath and gritted her teeth. At least she was here now. Maybe she could end this quickly.

But Sasha wasn't alone. Once she landed in the meadow, seven other vampires touched down as well, all of them snarling and showing their fangs. They weren't the creepy, disheveled lot of bloodsuckers she was used to seeing at the homes she'd frequented on hunts lately. No, these were the beautiful kind, the *Vampire Diaries* meets *Twilight* kind that would've taken her breath away if she would've still been breathing. Four sexy guys, three gorgeous women.

It was like couple's night at the goon academy and everyone wanted to look their best.

"Graham, are you seeing this?" she asked, praying he hadn't gone AWOL on her.

"Seeing what?" he asked. "I can't see you, Rachael. Where did you go?"

"You have got to be shitting me!" she said. Had she slipped through another portal into another realm? Is that what had happened the night before? "I've got vampire visitors times eight. I haven't moved! Maybe you can run your way into this alternate reality, too, if you take off now, but I don't think I can fight off all eight of them." She didn't even think she could fight off Sasha alone, for that matter.

Those heads were too gorgeous for exploding.... They probably wouldn't pop.

"I'll find you, Rachael. But it'll be difficult with the fog."

"Fog? What fog?" She took her eyes off Sasha long enough to check the weather and saw herself still standing in an open meadow. She had no idea what was going on, but it was creepy as hell, and Sasha Thornsby was bearing down on her, sharp teeth glistening in the moonlight.

It was time for Rachael to fight them off--or go down swinging.

FACE OFF

Rachael

SASHA and her band of goons had materialized out of nowhere, and now Rachael was all alone, readying herself to face them without the team. With Graham and half the team lost in the fog and the other half out looking for Sammi, there was no way to tell if she'd have any help.

Rachael dropped the book on the ground, assuming that wasn't what Sasha had come for anyway. Chances were, the vampire was there for her.

"Stop right there, Sasha or I'll explode your brain matter all over the trees behind you." Rachael had her hands up, hoping it would work like it had on the vampires in the basement at that creepy house, but she had a feeling Sasha was too strong for that.

The gorgeous ghoul laughed. "You know that won't work on us."

"Are you sure?" Rachael concentrated with all of her mind, staring at Sasha's head and putting all of her power into it. If she could get rid of Sasha, she could probably get the rest of them to scatter.

Sasha stopped in her tracks. Her eyes bulged, and she grabbed the sides of her head. Rachael couldn't believe it. Were her powers actually working against the vampire? Sasha began to screech, moving her head back and forth. Rachael continued to ramp up her powers, hoping at any moment Sasha's beautiful face would explode all over the place.

Instead, Sasha began to laugh. She put her hands down and raised her head. "Don't flatter yourself, newbie. You can't hurt me."

Furious at her trick, Rachael raised both of her hands and called upon her rage. This time, she saw the power leave her hands like an electric pulse. It hit Sasha in the chest and moved her backward several feet, similar to the way that it had the first time Rachael had blasted her in the road. But this time, Sasha was ready. She didn't go flying through the air. Instead, she blasted right back, and Rachael felt a burning sensation in her own chest.

With all of the power she could muster, she concentrated on shifting the blast away from herself, and the burning stopped as red beams of light dispersed around her. Sasha grunted and dropped her hands. Rachael had to do the same. She could feel the energy within her beginning to falter. She was going to have to take care of them the old fashioned way, with silver and wood. But she wasn't sure she'd be able to destroy all of them--or any of them for that matter.

Understanding the situation perfectly, Sasha rushed forward, her fangs barred and her claws ready to sink into Rachael's flesh. The hunter drew her blade, knowing the gun wouldn't do anything against vampires this strong. The others were moving toward her as well, and Rachael began to think she was about to be mulled.

Out of nowhere, Graham appeared next to her, as if he'd just cut through the fog Rachael was unable to see. Jared was there a second later, followed by Marcy, Ty, and a few of the students Rachael didn't know. The vampires were no longer able to rush her all at once, and a hand-to-hand battle ensued around her.

Rachael didn't have time to watch, though, as Sasha never slowed in her charge. She hit Rachael head on and knocked them both backward onto the plush carpet of grass.

Her blade stayed in her hand, and she swung it at the vampire as she did her best to sink her teeth into Rachael's neck. The hunter kicked up, catching the vampire in the stomach and giving her some space. Sasha's claws sank into Rachael's biceps, but she ignored the pain and brought the blade around, catching Sasha near her elbow. She screeched as blood squirted across the green grass, turning the scene into a garish Christmas display.

Sasha powered on, and it became apparent her goal was to sink her teeth into Rachael's neck. Being turned would be far worse than dying, in Rachael's opinion, so she couldn't let that happen. She continued to kick Sasha in the stomach, keeping her at bay, then, when Sasha lunged for her neck again, she rolled over so that she was on top of the vampire.

Rachael moved her hands out so she had the vampire by the wrists. Sasha continued to struggle against her, but her arm was weakened by the silver blade. The scent of burned flesh filled Rachael's nostrils as she realized she'd done more damage than she thought. If she could get to her stake, there was a possibility she could end this once and for all.

She'd need to scoot her knees up to hold one arm down while she pulled the stake from her interior pocket. Sasha was so strong, every time Rachael picked up her knees to move forward, the vampire pushed up off the ground and almost knocked her off entirely. This wasn't working. She'd have to find another way.

Gunfire rang out in front of her. Rachael watched as more of her teammates appeared. Sammi was with them, which was a relief. She saw Tripp and the others who'd been designated to go find the missing trainer. They were attempting to shoot something Rachael couldn't see, something behind her, but when the newly arrived hunters saw the scene around them, they quickly switched to combat mode.

The vampires were outnumbered for certain. Holding Sasha down, Rachael looked around and saw three or four break away, taking off for the trees. A few others were in precarious positions, like their leader. Graham had one pinned and pulled his stake as Rachael watched. The vampire shrieked and then went still. Two other bodies lay on the ground nearby.

Sasha knew she was the last one, and she'd soon have more than a dozen hunters bearing down on her. The vampire wrinkled up her face in determination, and the next thing she knew, Rachael was flying through the air. She landed on her bottom, hard, a few feet away, and Sasha jumped up.

Pissed that the vampire was getting away, Rachael leapt up and started to chase after her, but after a few steps, Rachael found herself standing in the middle of a thick fog. It was as if it had appeared from nowhere. She turned around but couldn't see her team anymore either.

Sasha was gone, and Rachael was all alone again. "Graham!" she shouted, praying he could hear her.

"Rachael! Walk toward my voice!" he said.

She could hear him, somewhere in that foggy mess in front of her. With a deep breath, Rachael took a few steps back the way she came.

The fog faded, and her team appeared in front of her, standing in the same peaceful meadow she'd been in all along, three vampire bodies on the ground. "How the hell...?"

"I don't know," Jared said, shaking his head. "I've never seen anything like it."

"Is everyone okay?" Graham asked, looking around.

A few people had scratches and cuts, but everyone was otherwise all right.

Turning to Sammi, Rachael asked, "What happened to you? Why were you screaming?"

The trainer's eyes bulged at the question, as if it had all just come back to her. "I saw something... I couldn't process."

"What was it?" Graham asked her.

Sammi's face went pale. "Chell. I saw Chell."

CHASING THE DEAD

Rachael

"WHAT DO you mean you saw Chell?" Marcy asked. She was standing next to Sammi and put her hand on her shoulder as she asked the other trainer what she was talking about.

Rachael assumed she already knew. She figured Sammi would say she'd seen her sister as a vampire, and that had been enough to freak her out and make her scream the way she had.

But that's not what Sammi said. Not exactly, anyway.

"I saw her, but it didn't look exactly like her, and she was… sucking the blood out of a deer! It was the most horrific thing I've ever seen in my life." She looked at Graham, and that made Rachael's eyes shift to him as well. He looked almost as unsettled as the trainer did.

"Sucking the blood out of a deer?" another hunter, Gill, asked. "What do you mean?"

"She was a vampire. When she looked up at me, she had blood dripping down her chin. Two-inch fangs protruded from her mouth. She snarled at me, and then she darted toward me, like I was going to be her next meal. I tried to reason with her, but it was like she knew who I was and didn't care."

"That's because it wasn't Chell--not exactly, anyway." Rachael said, not sure if she should be the one to explain or someone else.

"What do you mean?" Sammi asked, folding her arms and glaring at Rachael. "Don't you think I'd recognize my own fucking sister?"

"Yes, I do. But... that wasn't the Chell that was your sister."

"Are you going to say she's different now that she's a vampire? Because that's not helpful." Marcy glared at Rachael as she spoke.

Rachael had been under the impression Marcy wasn't so angry at her recently, but clearly she was wrong. "No, what I'm going to say is that this is Chell from another reality, an alternate reality. I know it sounds crazy, but it's true. That's what that book says, and that's what my father said when I spoke to him the other night, too."

"How do we know what your father said is true?" Ty asked, putting his hand on Sammi's shoulder. "Why didn't he stick around to talk to all of us?"

Blowing out a hot breath, Rachael attempted to explain but was having a hard time. "He couldn't. He said he had to go. Listen, I know it's hard to believe, but I came from an alternate reality, so I know first-hand that it's true. This Sasha, the one who just attacked us? She's not the one you locked in a cave back before Chell died. That Sasha is still there. This is one that was summoned from another real-ity. Chell was, too."

"Summoned by who?" Marcy wanted to know.

"By me--accidentally," Rachael admitted.

"We don't know that," Graham interjected, coming between Rachael and the rest of the team who looked extremely irritated now, save for Jared and Tripp who both already had an idea of what had transpired. "We're working off suppositions here."

"Why would you do that?" Sammi demanded, ignoring Graham.

"I was trying to bring Chell back. I certainly didn't mean to call Sasha. I don't know if that happened. But I wanted to bring the Chell you knew back, and I ended up bringing another one."

"That was just as much my fault as it was hers," Jared said, finally joining the conversation. "I told her a few ways I thought she could get our Chell back, and instead, this happened."

"You're just trying to protect her," Sammi said, shaking her head. "As if that will somehow get her to give a damn about you, Jared. It's pathetic."

Rachael's eyes widened. "Sammi, I know you're upset, but there's no reason to be a bitch!"

Everyone turned and looked at Rachael, shocked that she had stood up to Sammi. No one ever did that.

"I'm not trying to protect her, Sammi. It's true." Jared put his hands on his hips and looked Sammi in the eye.

She ran a hand through her hair and spun around. "All I know is, I came face to face with my sister out there. And she was a monster." She turned again. "If you guys knew that was a possibility, and you didn't tell me, you're all a bunch of assholes."

"We didn't know for sure," Graham said. "Rachael thought she saw her the other day, but no one else saw what she saw, and we thought there was a chance it was a mistake. We didn't want to tell anyone anything until we knew for sure."

"Lucky me I got to be the one to confirm it!" Sammi shrieked.

"That wouldn't have happened if you hadn't gotten out of the tree--against my orders." Graham's voice was calm, but it was clear he meant business.

"Listen, guys, it's been a long night, and we still have bodies to dispose of. Why don't we clean this mess up, head back to the academy, and figure the rest of this out tomorrow?" Tripp was the voice of reason, and everyone agreed that was for the best. Sammi was still glaring as she turned to help the team get rid of the dead vampires.

With a sigh, Rachael went back to where she'd left the book. She remembered dropping it on the grass as Sasha came at her. It wasn't where she thought it should be, so she looked around for a few more seconds, and then she started to freak out a little as she realized the book was gone.

SHE'S SMARTER THAN YOU THINK

Rachael

BACK AT THE ACADEMY, Rachael went to her room, alone. Graham had some work he wanted to do to try to figure out where Sasha might've disappeared to and why she might want the book. Rachael was ready to take a shower and collapse, but her mind wouldn't slow down either. Why did Sasha want that book? How had she materialized and disappeared so quickly? Where did that fog come from? And how did she stop someone so powerful?

She'd turned the shower on to heat up and was digging through her drawer looking for a specific pair of pajamas she wanted to wear when there was a knock on her door. It was locked so she had to go open it. With a sigh, she tossed her pajamas on the bed and pushed the drawer in, wondering who would be knocking at her door at almost 5:00 in the morning.

"Why did you lock me out?" Jazz asked as Rachael pulled the door open.

"I figured you were asleep. The fan's on," Rachael replied, letting her in.

"I was asleep, but I heard y'all come in. Your boots sound like a damn rhino comin' down the hallway wearing clodhoppers on its feet."

Rachael raised an eyebrow but didn't feel like defending herself or her footwear to the girl. "What do you want, Jazz?" she asked as her friend stepped in.

"I wanna know how it went. Did you get her?"

Rachael scoffed and moved back into the bedroom. Jazz followed her. "No, we didn't get her. It didn't go well. We lost the book, too."

"You what now?" Jazz asked, flopping down on the bed. "How'd that happen?"

"She took it. I dropped it so we could fight, and somehow, one of them snatched it before they disappeared into a fog that seemed to come and go as it pleased. It was weird, Jazz. It was like we were walking in and out of realms."

"What do you mean?" Her eyebrows were so high, they were practically on the back of her head.

"I mean… I was standing in the field with trees all around me where the team was waiting, but they saw a fog roll in, one I couldn't see, and then Sasha showed up, along with a team of her goons. We started fighting. Graham and some of the others just seemed to be there all of a sudden. From their perspective, they'd run through a thick fog. The whole thing was bizarre to say the least." She shook her head, not sure how else to explain it.

"That sounds like what your dad was talking about in the chapter about leaping," she said.

"Leaping?" Rachael wasn't sure she'd even seen a chapter about that. "What's that?"

"I'd say grab the book and look it up, but I guess you can't do that." She rolled her eyes.

"We took pictures of every page before we left, so I could read it. But right now I'm going to take a shower. You could go talk to Jared and Graham about it, if you think you know enough about it to help them figure out what Sasha was up to."

"It's pretty simple." Jazz continued to talk to her as if she hadn't said she was about to take a shower. "Sasha can use her power to create a hole in her current reality and leap through to a different location in the same reality. She can't go back to where she came from because she doesn't have the ability to go back to her original realm. But she is strong enough to leap through to another place."

Rachael stared at her for a moment. "Does she have any control over where she ends up?"

"That depends. The book says some are strong enough to direct a leap and others aren't. Either way, you'll have to figure out a way to tether her to the same spot if you want to keep her from leaping long enough to destroy her."

"Tether her?" Rachael asked, folding her arms. "How do I do that?"

Jazz let out a loud sigh and folded her arms. "Did you read anything in that book?"

"No, not really." Rachael admitted. "I gave it to Jared to read. Then, I gave it to you."

"To tether her, you need something of hers, something important."

"Like, what? Her teddy bear?" Again, Rachael was baffled.

"No, like… a piece of jewelry that's important to her. Or maybe even something that's literally hers--blood, hair, an appendage."

Wrinkling her nose, Rachael envisioned herself slicing Sasha's hand off. "Then what?"

"Then, you can tether it to wherever you are by securing it to your person."

"So… I have someone sew her severed hand onto my arm?" She smirked, knowing that would get an eye roll out of Jazz, which it did.

"No. I think putting it in an interior pocket in your jacket should be enough. It won't last forever. She'll figure out a way to cut the tether. But it will prevent her from breaking away from the location so quickly."

Rachael would need to think about all of that for a while. "Okay-- good to know. Thank you. I need to go take a shower now."

"That's all I get? A quick thank you?"

Frustrated, Rachael asked, "What do you want? A hug? A kiss? My first born?"

"No! I wanna go with you!"

"Into the shower??"

Jazz rolled her eyes yet again.

Rachael scoffed, knowing she meant on a hunt. "You know I have no control over that."

"You have influences. See if you can talk him into it."

"Jazz, what if you get out there and something happens to you? I'll never forgive myself."

"Nothing's going to happen to me. I can defend myself."

"Is your magic even working?" The last Rachael had seen, Jazz's magic was more like a flicker than a flame.

Instead of answering, she created a ball of fire in her hands. She stretched her hands apart, and the flame grew larger.

"That is impressive," Rachael admitted. "Okay--I'll ask." She headed toward the bathroom.

"You better--or I'll burn your head off!" Jazz shouted after her.

Rachael laughed, imagining Jazz throwing a large fireball at her head. It would be nice to have Jazz on the battlefield, but it would also be scary. Still, if she'd been there that night, maybe she would've been able to help Rachael tether Sasha so that she could've ended all of this tonight.

The sooner it was over, the better. She'd definitely talk to Graham about Jazz coming with them next time. But for now, she was taking a shower and going to sleep. Unfortunately, vampires would still be there when she woke up.

GET IT BACK

Rachael

"HOW DO we get her back to tether her if she already has the book?" Jared was asking later that afternoon when Graham called a meeting to talk about Jazz's concerns.

"If she still wants Rachael, it shouldn't be so hard," Graham pointed out.

"Or we could, you know, hunt her," Sammi said with a sarcastic eye roll. "That's kind of our job anyhow."

Jared narrowed his eyes at her. "I'm aware of that, Sammi, but if she can jump through portals, that might make it a little more challenging."

"I think we can draw her back out," Rachael said, though she wasn't exactly sure why she felt that way. "She said she wanted to kill me, and that was before we even had the book, so she must've wanted me first."

"That was before we knew we had the book. Who knows when it was actually placed in the library." Marcy looked almost as irritated as Sammi did.

"We won't know until we try," Rachael said with a shrug. "If we can't get her to show up of her own accord, then we'll have to track her down."

"Are we sure this tethering thing will even work?" Sammi asked.

Everyone turned to look at Jazz then. This was her first meeting with the hunters, and despite her usual confidence, she looked nervous. "It will work," she said with a nod. "We just have to make sure we do it right. And once she's tethered, we have to destroy her before she breaks the bind."

"And how does she do that?" Jared used a lot kinder tone than Sammi had when she asked her previous question.

"The book says she can break the bind by using her power to illuminate the tether and cutting it with a blade of steel."

All of them had pictures of the book on their phones now, so Jared pulled his out and opened it. "Where does it say that, exactly, Jazz?"

"Page two seventy-eight, paragraph three," she replied with an eye roll that told Rachael she was tired of everyone questioning her ability to read.

Others pulled out their phones, too. Rachael had gone over all of this with Jazz when she'd woken up, after her shower, so she'd already read it. It seemed like Jazz was able to decipher meaning from the poetic phrasing of the book better than she could herself.

Jared read the paragraph aloud, "A bind that ties one to the world around can be severed by a splice through the tethering with a blade of strongest resolve. Light must guide the way or else the bind will remain hidden. The strongest of powers called upon will set the tether aglow. Only then can the enchantment be broken and the captive set free to leap through tears in the veil." He looked up then and made eye contact with Jazz.

"See?" she said with a shrug. "Blade of steel. Light it up with her powers, cut it. Free to portal jump again."

The room was silent for a moment as the others contemplated whether or not Jazz had missed anything. It didn't seem that way to Rachael. As far as she could tell, Jazz was spot on.

"Will this work on the others as well?" Sammi asked. It wasn't clear whether or not she wanted Jazz's answer to be affirmative or not, but it was obvious why she was asking. Could they use this method to trap Chell here so that she could be destroyed? Would Sammi be able to watch her older sister die again?

"It only works on vampires that came from other worlds," Jazz said. "They can open portals and other vampires can leap through, but the vampires who originated in our world can't open portals anyway."

"So, yes," Rachael said, looking at Sammi. "It will hold Chell here as well."

"And you're sure… that's not my actual sister?" she asked, her voice much softer than normal, almost breaking on the last part of the question.

"I'm sure," Rachael said with a nod. "It couldn't possibly be your sister."

"Sammi, our Chell's gone. Nothing is going to bring her back." Graham leaned over and put his hand on Sammi's knee.

She had tears in her eyes as she nodded. "Whoever has to do that job…."

"I'll do it," Jazz said. "I didn't know her. I don't think anyone who knew the real Chell should have to do it. And Rachael will be busy with Sasha."

"What makes you think you're strong enough to do that?" Marcy asked her. "I've seen your power and magic during training, and it's not that impressive."

"With all due respect, Ms. Marcy, I was just tryin' to help. You don't have to be a bitch," Jazz replied with her arms folded.

Rachael's eyes widened, and she tried not to laugh, but a few of her other teammates let out a chuckle.

Marcy wasn't amused. "I wasn't trying to be a bitch, Jasmine. I was reminding you that you haven't even been on an observation hunt yet, so maybe you shouldn't get ahead of yourself."

"Jazz, I appreciate the offer," Graham said, his tone implying they were done arguing about it. "I may need your help, but I'll do it."

"You can't do that, Graham," Sammi said. "How could you possibly look her in the eye and destroy her?"

"Because, she's not Chell. She's a vampire. My job is to destroy vampires. Regardless of what they look like, they have to be destroyed. I'm not saying it'll be easy, but I can do it. And I will do it."

Rachael wanted to believe that Graham was strong enough to destroy Chell, but she didn't know if he could do it or not. In the end, it would be better if Jazz was there to finish it if need be. She might not be as powerful as the Chell from this world, but she was determined, especially after Marcy's taunt.

"Then it's settled. We'll draw them out, tether them, and destroy them. Piece of cake," Tripp said with a shrug.

"Yep. Easy as pie," Rachael said, shaking her head. All of them knew there would be nothing easy about this mission, but it was necessary, and they'd have to make it work because as long as Sasha and this new Chell were out there, they were all in danger.

ANOTHER TRICK

Rachael

IT WAS FAR TOO SOON for Rachael to find herself standing out in the open alone. This time, she wasn't in a lovely meadow full of plush green grass, though. She was standing amidst a ton of heavy boulders that had somehow wound up in the middle of Pennsylvania farmland, boulders where a whole bunch of men had died during the Civil War. She looked around at the massive rocks and thought it was no wonder this place had been called the Devil's Den.

Her team was scattered around the area. Some were up in trees again, others waiting in the shadows on motorcycles. A few were further down in the rocks. Jazz was there, but since they'd okayed her to come along, Graham had caved and brought Rex, Karma, Tony, and Georgia, too; basically anyone from Rachael's class who asked to go and was somewhat ready. He'd warned them to stay back and stay out of the fray if at all possible, but Rachael knew that Jazz at least would end up in the middle of things if there was a fight.

And if Sasha showed up, there would be a fight.

Why would she come, though? She'd have to know what she was

getting herself into. Rachael told herself that she would simply try to lure the vampire out into the open under the pretenses that she wanted a chance to get the book back, but Sasha had to know it would be more than that.

The only reason the vampire would come would be if she thought she could end Rachael. That would be a difficult task to do since Sasha would have to know that Rachael wouldn't be waiting alone. Of course, if she managed to pull her into a portal, or whatever she'd done last time to obscure her from her team, that would make it easier on Sasha.

The hunter was pacing back and forth on the flat ground in front of the mammoth rocks. Some of the dark brown stones were as big as a compact car. She wondered if a glacier had pushed them all here or if the devil himself really had spit them up from the bowels of hell.

As she paced, she tried to keep her thoughts on Sasha, as if she could call out to her and bring her there through her sheer willpower. It had worked the other night, but then, Rachael had had something Sasha wanted. Why she wanted it, she still couldn't say, unless she just didn't want Rachael to have it. There had to be more to it, though, more they hadn't gotten a chance to figure out since they'd been so focused on figuring out how to tether Sasha.

Rachael considered pulling her phone out and going over the book while she was standing there, trying to figure out Sasha's purpose for snatching it, but she knew any sort of distraction could cost her precious seconds, so she didn't do it. Instead, she used all of her mental energy to stay focused on calling the vampire out.

Two hours later, Rachael was beginning to think it would be best to give it up for the night and try again at another time when she heard footsteps on the large rocks to her left.

Looking up, she saw the full moon before she saw the vampire standing there, her long red hair blowing out behind her, the book held in her hand as if it were a piece of trash she was about to throw away or didn't care if she lost.

Instinctively, Rachael's eyes traced her surroundings, looking for other predators, but she saw no one. "Can you see this?" she asked Graham over the radio.

"See what?" he asked.

Blowing out a sigh, she said, "Sasha is here. Right there on the rocks. Where I'm looking. Can you see me?"

"I can see you, but I don't see her. Where?"

Before she could answer, Sasha started moving, jumping down from one giant boulder to the next with ease as she slowly made her way to Rachael. She kept her distance, though, even once her feet had touched down on the ground, Sasha was still at least twenty yards away.

"Are you alone?" Rachael asked her.

Sasha shrugged and turned her head slightly. "Do you see anyone else?"

"No, but no one else can see you either. How are you doing that?"

Sasha laughed. It was a mix between a cackle and a hearty chuckle a friend might let loose over lunch. "Why would I tell you that? You can have your book back now. I don't need it anymore."

She tossed it over, and Rachael caught it, but she didn't want to keep it in her hands because she'd need them to fight if things came to that. She hoped they did. Seeing Sasha standing there made her hunter blood begin to boil, and she wanted to get into it already.

"We aren't fighting here," Sasha said, as if she was reading her mind. "I'm not stupid. I know you understand what has to be done."

"What are you talking about?" Rachael truly was confused.

"The tether," Sasha said, her now empty hands on her hips. "I know that's what you intend to do. But if you want to tether me, you're going to have to catch me first."

As soon as she finished speaking, Sasha waved her arm and a large ball of purple light began to glow near the rocks on her left, Rachael's right. The hunter watched in shock as the lights twirled and then an opening spread between them so that the purple lights had formed a glowing ring around what looked like a doorway.

"Why would I do that?" Rachael asked, watching Sasha take a few steps closer to the opening.

"Do you want to end this?" she asked. "Or do you want to keep chasing me forever?"

Rachael considered her choices. It wasn't as if she'd been chasing Sasha for all that long to begin with. After all, it had only been a few months. Surely, she could put up with chasing her a bit longer before she went diving into a hole that led to who knows where....

She was just about to tell her to go to hell when a commotion coming from her left had her head swiveling around. It was Chell--the vampire version--running fast, and behind her, Sammi came flying at full-speed, too. Where they'd come from, Rachael wasn't sure, but she had a feeling it was more of Sasha's tricks obscuring her view.

Chell ran straight for the hole, and without a second thought, Sammi went through, too. "Sammi!" Rachael screamed. "Son of a bitch," she muttered as Sammi disappeared.

Sasha laughed again, realizing she had her now. There was no way Rachael could let Sammi go alone, even if she wasn't a fan of the woman.

As Sasha moved toward the hole, Rachael followed, cursing under her breath. This was a bad idea.

She forged ahead, though, holding her breath like she was diving under water, and went through, praying she didn't find her own devil's den on the other side.

PORTAL

Rachael

RACHAEL EXPECTED WALKING through the portal to be something like it appeared in the movies, like a whooshing noise, blowing wind, disorienting, something…. But it wasn't anything like that. She was simply running through Devil's Den one moment and then through a field a second later.

Ahead of her, she saw Sasha sprinting away, but the vampire only took a few steps before she stopped, turned, and looked right at her. She couldn't see Sammi and Chell, but then, she realized they were in a situation where that fog she couldn't see was obstructing everything except for herself and Sasha.

And Graham who came running in a few seconds behind her. Sasha wasn't happy to see him. Her face morphed from a grimace to a menacing frown. It was clear that she intended to face Rachael one on one, but now she'd have to deal with Graham, too.

"It's closed, isn't it?" Rachael asked, meaning the portal they'd just come through. "So you wanted it to be just me and you, but now Graham's here, too."

"I can handle that," Sasha said with a shrug. "I was just hoping to deal with you alone. Well, not exactly alone."

Out of nowhere, a clan of vampires appeared around them, forming a tight circle, shoulder to shoulder. Rachael's eyes bulged as she realized they had to be outnumbered by at least twenty to one as the monsters began to cackle and whoop with glee.

"Holy shit," Graham muttered.

There wasn't any time for Rachael to stand there and calculate the odds. She had to act fast before Sasha and her team of goons had a chance to take the first swing.

Just as she had in the basement, Rachael put all of her energy into exploding the heads of the vampires around her. She was fully aware that there wasn't much chance that she'd be able to get all of them, as she had the weak bastards the last time she managed to take out a group even larger than this, but she hoped that she could at least end a few of them and even their numbers a bit.

Sasha began to laugh as Rachael concentrated her energy into the task, but it didn't take long at all for the effects to take shape. A few screams behind them had Graham turning around, but Rachael didn't want to break her concentration. A shout to her left and another two to her right let her know she was at least making some progress.

No longer content to stand back and watch her army be destroyed, Sasha moved forward, with a shriek of hatred. Rachael had to break her concentration to defend herself, but she did note that she'd taken out about six of the vampires Sasha had assembled. While they were still grossly outnumbered, at least it wasn't as bad as it had been before.

Graham turned so that his back was toward hers. The attack came from all sides at once. Rachael had little trouble fending off the attacks from either side of her with a quick blast from her gun in each direction. It didn't end those vampires, but it did send them flying, and gave her more time so she could deal with them in turn. The real problem was standing in front of her. Sasha had her claws out and her fangs had dropped as she lunged at Rachael.

"We can't do this," Graham said, fighting off two or three vampires behind her as Rachael took a kick at Sasha. "We're going to need more help."

"No one else came through the portal, though," Rachael reminded him.

"Except for--"

Before he could complete the sentence, a rain of gunfire sprinkled down on the vampires around them, sending many of them running for cover. Rachael looked up to see Sammi was back, and she was packing heat. It looked like she had some sort of sawed off shot-gun that shot like a machine gun. That evened things up, but it didn't look like many of the vampires were staying down as a result of being shot. They'd have to do more.

Sasha came at her again. At least now, Rachael would be able to concentrate solely on Sasha. She was up from the kick and coming back at her. The vampire swung her claws at Rachael, catching her in the cheek. Rachael pooled her light in her hand and shot out with it. Sending a streak of lightning flying at the vampire, she knocked Sasha back again, just in time to defend herself from another vampire who was coming at her from her right.

Rachael brought her elbow around and caught the monster in the jaw, sending her head back. She then pulled her blade from her belt and jabbed it into the vampire's neck. That one wouldn't be getting up again.

But Sasha was back now, more furious than ever. Sammi's bullets had done as much damage as she was going to with the gun. The trainer dropped her weapon and came sprinting over, pulling a long blade as she came. Rachael couldn't watch the trainer and defend herself against Sasha, but she was glad that Sammi was on their side.

Sasha was swinging at her again. With her cheek still bleeding, Rachael was in no mood to take another scratch, so she dodged out of the way, bringing her leg up and catching her in the back of the knee. Sasha yelped as her leg crumpled. Rachael moved around behind her, and as Sasha was attempting to get back up, Rachael leapt on her back, wrapping her arm around the vampire's neck. She placed the other hand on top of her head, wanting to end this once and for all.

Sammi and Graham were still grossly outnumbered. There were at least ten more vampires than there were hunters, not counting herself and Sasha, but the urge to tear Sasha's head off was overwhelming, and Rachael wanted to be done with her.

Sasha was flailing, trying to get her off. Rachael still had her blade in the hand that was around Sasha's neck. She tried to change her grip so she could slice through the vampire's throat, but with Sasha struggling to kick her off, she couldn't get her hand around, and the blade slid from her fingers, landing on the ground.

Another vampire came to Sasha's assistance, maneuvering behind Rachael. She kicked out at the woman, but she lost her balance, and Sasha elbowed her, and Rachael went flying. As she went sailing away from Sasha, she grabbed hold of her long red hair, and pulled a chunk of it out of the vampire's head.

Landing on her feet, Rachael readied herself to go back at Sasha, but the vampire had had enough, at least for now. She made a rumbling noise in her throat, and all of the vampires disengaged, backing away from the three hunters who were all bleeding and struggling to catch their breath.

A few steps later, the vampires were gone, and Rachael found herself staring at what looked like a wide open field that was really just a hallucination.

Wiping blood off her face onto her sleeve, Rachael took a few deep breaths and moved toward her team members. "You guys okay?"

"Peachy." Sammi said, shaking her head. "Chell got away."

"So did Sasha, obviously." Rachael noted. But she did have a chunk of her hair. She didn't get to try to do the tethering like Jazz had recommended, but at least she had something important to help do it next time.

"How the hell do we get home?" Graham asked.

Rachael's eyes widened. "I have no fucking idea."

GET OUT!

Rachael

Trying to read the pictures of the book on her phone was difficult, especially since Rachael's hands were shaking. The three of them had been searching for any signs of an opening that might take them back to their world for at least an hour, but so far, all it had gotten any of them was a lot of cursing from Sammi.

"I can't find anything," Rachael said, slamming her phone down against her leg in frustration.

"Let me see it," Sammi insisted, practically snatching the phone out of her hand.

Rachael grimaced but let her have it. The book was making little sense at the moment, and she had to wonder if it was something like what had happened when Jared was attempting to read it. Was the fact that they were in another world somehow changing what her dad had written?

"What the hell language is this anyway?" Sammi asked. "It's not even written in complete sentences!"

"Thank you," Rachael replied, knowing Sammi's statement wasn't meant to validate her thoughts but still appreciating it.

"This is bullshit!" She started to throw the phone, but Graham took it away from her and handed it back to Rachael.

"Thank you," she said again, putting her phone into her pocket because it wasn't doing them any good anyway. She'd even tried calling Jazz, but the girl's number was no longer in her phone. Probably because she didn't exist in this world.

Sammi continued to swear, walking around in circles, like a hole was just going to appear if she walked around enough. "Do I need to remind you that the reason the three of us are here is because you chased Chell through the portal opening?" Graham asked her after she declared everything was "bullshit" again.

"Go to hell, Graham!" she said. "I know why we're here. If it was your fucking sister, maybe you'd want to catch her, too."

"Well, it was my fucking fiancée and I didn't want to chase her in here," he retaliated.

"No, just your current fucking girlfriend can get you to come here, huh?"

"She came here to try to save your sorry ass!" Graham shouted.

"Stop!" Rachael said, sticking her hands up between them. "It doesn't matter. What matters is finding a way out of here and back to where we belong. If the book doesn't help, maybe I can write us back to Silverwood."

"Hell, no!" Sammi declared. "That's what created all of these problems in the first place. If you didn't think you could write yourself a new existence, none of this would've happened to begin with."

"Do you have a better idea?" Rachael asked her, still trying to stay calm. She really didn't want to fight with Sammi or anyone at this point, but the woman was getting on her last nerve, and months' worth of frustration were beginning to bubble to the surface.

Sammi didn't say anything, only glared at her, and Rachael took that as a no. "Maybe... I can use my powers to open a portal?" She looked at Graham for confirmation, her eyebrows raised in expectation of confirmation.

"You think?" He didn't sound as hopeful as she would've liked.

"I don't know. What else can we do?"

He shook his head. "I can't think of anything."

"Why was Sasha able to leave?" Sammi asked, her voice showing how angry she still was. "I thought you were supposed to tether her or some kinda shit."

"I tried, but apparently, there's more that has to be done than just pulling out a chunk of her hair."

"Seriously? Don't you think you should've figured that out before we went to try to tether her?"

"Yeah, probably. But... I thought that's all I had to do. At least when we were in the other world, Jazz could've walked me through it. But now we're here, and for all I know, it only works in certain worlds."

Sammi rolled her eyes and walked away. Rachael was tempted to try exploding her head--but she didn't.

Instead, she moved away from the others, too, and decided to give her powers a try. She had no idea how they might work when it came to opening a portal, but she hadn't known she could blow up vampires' heads until she'd done that either. It would take an awful lot of luck for her to open a portal back into the world where she wanted to be, but she had to try. She couldn't stay here much longer, not with Sammi anyway.

Raising her hands, Rachael called on her power, pooling the blue light into her palms before she had a concentration of power in her hands. Then, with all of her thoughts focused on opening a portal back to their world, she sent the stream of light out into an open space, and gave it everything she had.

The light danced and glowed, ebbing and flowing, potentially moved by the breeze but seeming to take on an energy of its own, moving in space. For what seemed like ten minutes, Rachael did her best to try to stretch the light into an opening, but all that seemed to be happening was her powers were draining.

"You should stop before we discover this is all a ruse, and Sasha shows back up to fight, now that your powers are mostly gone," Graham advised.

"I have to be able to do this," she argued, not looking away from her work to face him.

"Let's go back to the book. Maybe it'll adjust and be useful now that it's been here a while." She knew he was right, that she was wasting energy and not accomplishing anything. Giving up seemed like she had failed, though. She kept her hands up, trying to focus, but at the moment, all she could think about was Graham's hand on her shoulder. "Thank you, by the way, for coming after me. I didn't even know you were there until I was in this field."

"I just made it through before the portal closed," he said. "Of course, I'd come with you." He kissed the top of her head and then urged her, "Stop, Rachael. Let it go."

She let out a sigh and started to drop her hands, but then, something different began to appear in front of her. Rather than the blue lights twinkling, there was a black ring forming, and then the air started to peel back away from the ring, and Rachael found herself peering into another place.

Giant boulders dotted the landscape. Then, she made out forms beyond the initial ring. "Devil's Den!" Sammi shouted. "You did it!" She didn't wait on Rachael and Graham but ran through the hole.

"God, I hope she's right, and that's our way home," Graham said. "Come on."

With a deep breath, Rachael stepped through, praying things were back to normal now--well, not *normal* normal, but her new normal.

And hopefully those forms she saw were her friends and not another set of vampires because Rachael was too tired to fight.

FINALLY OUT

Rachael

"THERE YOU ARE!" Jazz said as the three of them stepped through. Rachael ran to her and wrapped her arms around her friend, glad to see her, even if she did have a sarcastic look in her eyes. "Damn, we've been searching for y'all for hours."

"What?" Rachael asked, stepping back. "What are you talking about? We haven't been gone that long."

"Maybe not to you, but it's almost four in the morning here. Took me forever to find you." She shook her head, and Rachael noticed Rex standing next to her, holding the book.

"Wait--you found us? I didn't open the portal?"

"Hell, no," Jazz said, folding her arms. "I found you, girl. Rex and I been lookin' through that book, tryin' to figure out how to get that damn portal open. We almost let some big ass dinosaurs through. That was a close one."

Rachael looked at Rex and then the other faces. Lots of people were eagerly telling Sammi and Graham welcome back but hadn't interrupted Rachael and Jazz. She could tell by Rex's expression that

Jazz wasn't bullshitting her. For once. "Well, thanks for not giving up on us."

"When you gonna learn not to go through portals?" Jazz asked, shaking her head.

"What was I supposed to do? I couldn't let Sammi go by herself."

"Why not?" Jazz and Sammi asked at the same time. They both glared at each other.

Jazz continued. "She wouldn't have done the same for you."

"I didn't ask you to come after me." Sammi continued to glare at both of them.

"Did you get her?" Jared asked, interrupting.

Rachael assumed he was talking to her about Sasha and not to Sammi about Chell. "No, we got a few of her lackeys, but not her."

"Lackeys? What do you mean?" he asked, taking a few steps closer to her.

"She had a mob waiting for me," Rachael explained, "ready to jump me. She wasn't expecting anyone else to go through, I guess. Anyway, I exploded some of them, and the three of us took out some more, but we didn't get Sasha. Or Chell."

"Did you try the tether?" Jazz asked. "Why didn't you tether her?"

"I tried. Sort of." Rachael pulled the handful of red hair out of her pocket. "It didn't go as planned."

"Damn, you got her hair, and you didn't do it?"

"I wanted to. I don't know what I'm supposed to do with it once I have the artifact, Jazz. I thought she'd just… be tethered."

"No, you gotta command her to stay there."

"How was I supposed to know that?"

"Might've been a good thing to mention before we dragged her ass out tonight." Marcy looked just as irritated as Rachael felt, but she assumed that comment was intended for her and turned to glare at the trainer.

"Well, at least I have her hair for next time. It will work next time, won't it? If I command her, and I have her hair on my person?"

"Hell if I know. I'm just making this shit up as I go along." Jazz was clearly irritated as she glared at everyone else except for Rex. "Come on, let's go home."

She turned and headed toward the SUVs, which were parked over a mile away so as not to draw attention to them from anyone, including the vampires. All of the students and some of the others turned to follow Jazz, like she was their new leader.

Rachael sought Graham's eyes out of the crowd. He shrugged and went along, as if Jazz had just become the boss of him as well. Not that Rachael didn't want to leave, but she had to wonder if maybe something didn't shift when Jazz opened that portal. Had the girl somehow changed things so that she was the head of the group now? Or were people just afraid to argue with her because of her fresh mouth?

Either way, Rachael fell into step, thankful that Graham came up behind her and slipped his hand into hers. At least that hadn't changed…. Jazz may have somehow managed to make herself the leader, but Graham was still her man, and that was most important to Rachael.

She'd tucked Sasha's hair back into the interior pocket of her jacket, and she hoped the next time she got a chance to tether the vampire she would be able to. But she didn't want to have to go out looking for the monster again. Hopefully, next time they met, it would be without tricks or games. And Rachael would end that bitch once and for all.

NOW WHAT?

Rachael

BACK IN HER ROOM, Rachael put the book in what she hoped was a safe place in her closet and then sat down next to Graham on the couch. Even though she was exhausted and they both needed to sleep, she had so many questions swarming around in her brain, she wanted to talk it out first.

"What's the deal with Jazz?" he asked, which was the prevalent question on her mind as well.

"I don't know," Rachael admitted. The fan next door was whirring, which made her assume they wouldn't be overheard. "She seemed to have command of everyone after we left, and even when we came back, she was giving orders. I thought maybe I'd messed up the world again."

"No, I just didn't want to argue with her, and we needed to leave anyway," he said, running a hand through his hair. "I guess I'll have to have a little talk with her later."

"She does seem to have a deeper understanding of the book than anyone else, which seems odd to me. My dad wrote it--for me. Why doesn't it make more sense to me than to her?"

"That I can't tell you, unless she happens to have some sort of superpower that relates to being able to decipher an ever-evolving book written in another realm about how to stop things from changing in our own world. It doesn't make a whole lot of sense, but then, what does anymore?"

She could tell he was just as exhausted as she was. "I wish there was a way we could get Sasha to come out on our own terms, but it seems every time we try that, she turns it into something she has control of that we don't."

"That's what vampires do," Graham said with a deep sigh. He ran his hand through Rachael's hair. "We're going to have to do something about Sammi, too. She endangered all of us tonight."

"Yep, and didn't even seem thankful that we followed after her either. Next time, maybe I'll just let her go."

He smirked at her. "We've got a lot to sort out," Graham said, taking her hand and putting it in his lap. "But for now, I think we should get some rest and talk about it tomorrow."

Rachael agreed with that. "What do I do with this?" she asked, reaching into her pocket and pulling out the strands of red hair she'd yanked out of Sasha's head. There were about ten of them, long, bright red, and silky. "I wish I knew what kind of conditioner this bitch uses."

"Blood," Graham said. Rachael raised an eyebrow, and he grinned at her, but she figured he might just be right. "I would put that in a locket or something you can easily keep track of."

"I was thinking a Ziplock bag, but your idea sounds a little more sophisticated." She rolled her eyes, making him laugh again, and went over to her jewelry box.

She had an empty locket, one that she'd gotten for her birthday a few years ago from someone--an aunt, maybe?--she couldn't even remember. The idea of wearing Sasha's hair around her neck as if it was important to her seemed odd, but she didn't know what else to do with a locket. So she put the hair inside, which took some doing since it didn't want to cooperate, and then hooked the locket around her neck. She glanced down at it and then stared at herself in the mirror. The pendant was a circular shape with spirals and an odd pattern on it. At least it wasn't a heart….

Graham came up behind her, his hands on her hips, and she leaned back into him, admiring how handsome he was in the mirror. His breath was a hot breeze against her cheek. "Ready to go to bed?" he asked, and she was suddenly very aware that sleeping was no longer his priority.

Rachael spun in his arms and found his mouth as he made short work of getting off her jacket. Their kisses deepened, and he pulled her across the room over to her bed. Even with all the chaos going on in the world, having Graham's arms around her made Rachael feel safe and protected. She couldn't imagine ever going back to a reality that he wasn't part of. No matter what else happened, wherever she might end up, or who she might have to kill, as long as Graham was with her, she could handle it all.

He took his time, peeling off her clothes as she did the same for him, their kisses lengthening as their hands continued to roam one another.

Once they were both naked, Graham lying beside her on the bed, he whispered in her ear, "I'm really impressed with how you took control tonight."

She didn't want to think about the battle. She only wanted to think about his hand that was on her breast, teasing her nipple into a hardened peak. But she smiled and brushed his hair back in thanks.

"Why don't you take control in here, too?" Graham asked her.

Rachael's initial response was that she was too tired for that, but when he lay on his back next to her, his hand sliding to her hip to tug her over to him, she went.

He was already hard, standing at attention, and Rachael could feel her own juices slipping down her thighs, so mounting him completely was no problem. She settled over him with a moan and looked into his lavender eyes.

As Rachael began to move her hips back and forth, slow, deep, grinding, Graham kept one hand on her breast and slid the other between her folds.

He teased her at first, touching everything but her most sensitive spot, but once he made contact with her there, Rachael had no choice but to pick up the pace. She went from a leisurely, sensual ride to a quick, erotic, spastic jackhammering motion as he flicked and rubbed against her.

Waves of pleasure rippled through her body as Rachael tipped her head back and moaned so loudly, everyone in the building might have heard it, and as she felt herself slip over the edge, she reached behind her to find Graham's balls and ran her fingers across them until he was right there with her.

Taking hold of her hips, he steadied both of them as he filled her with his essence. Rachael felt the heat spreading inside of her.

With a deep breath, she threw her leg over the top of him to dismount and collapsed next to him on the pillow. Graham pulled her face over to him and kissed her deeply.

Whatever world they were in now, she wanted to stay forever.

HOW IS THIS POSSIBLE?

Rachael

IT WAS SUPPOSED to be a routine hunt, nothing to do with Sasha or Chell or anyone they were aware of, but from the moment Rachael stepped into the old, abandoned warehouse on the outskirts of Baltimore, she knew something was off.

At first, it was just a feeling deep in her gut that things were about to get more dangerous, but when the locket she'd taken to wearing around her neck began to glow, she knew Sasha had to be nearby.

They'd brought in a large team, including some of the students, because the warehouse was huge, and no one knew for sure how many vampires they might find there. Recent activity had a lot of the other teams Graham's people would normally call in all tied up with other jobs, so he'd had to rely on bringing hunters who otherwise wouldn't be considered ready.

Rachael thought they were, though, especially the upperclassmen who'd been to several observational hunts. Jazz had calmed down in the last few weeks since she'd basically tried to take over the hunt at

Devil's Den. Graham and Jared had both spoken to her, but it had been Sammi who'd put her in her place.

Still, Jazz was with them now, and since Rachael was beginning to think she might actually have a chance to tether Sasha this time, she was glad the expert was in her ear and not too far away, even though she wasn't in the same group as Rachael.

The second story wasn't as large as the story below them, but it was crowded with crates and old boxes filled with who knows what. Rachael was with Graham, Jared, and Ty, and with every step she took, she felt as if the four of them were not alone.

Her locket was glowing so brightly now, it caught the attention of her teammates. "What the hell is wrong with that thing?" Ty asked. "You've got a freaking beacon around your neck."

Rachael dropped it down inside of her shirt, but since the T-shirt she had on beneath her leather jacket was white, it didn't help too much. "I don't know what's going on with it, but it can't be good," she admitted.

"That didn't help much." Ty shook his head.

"I realize that," Rachael said, rolling her eyes at him.

"Has it ever done that before?" Jared asked her.

"Not that I've noticed." She had only been on a few hunts since she'd taken the strands of Sasha's hair and put them in the locket in question. She probably would've seen it if the locket had begun to glow before. The fact that she hadn't seen Sasha since she'd ripped several strands of her hair out also meant that if the glowing was related to the vampire, as Rachael believed it had to be, then there would've been no reason for it to start glowing until now, assuming the bloodsucker was out there somewhere.

"We've got movement on floor one," Tripp said into her ear. A few seconds later, all hell broke loose beneath them. Rachael could hear a commotion as her teammates moved in to destroy the vampires. Hopefully, no one on her side would get hurt.

"Marcy, can you send some people down to help?" Graham asked of the trainer he'd put in charge on top of the roof.

"Affirmative. Sending five."

"Thanks." Graham caught Jared's eyes, and Rachael saw the two of them calculating whether or not that would be enough.

She wondered if they were about to need some backup themselves. So far, nothing was moving up here, but that didn't mean that they weren't about to encounter the queen mother of all vampires.

Graham signaled for the four of them to split up, and Rachael followed his orders, even though the hairs on the back of her neck were beginning to stand up. She found herself walking between rows of crates stacked so high, she couldn't see over them. There wasn't much room to maneuver here, though she could've turned around if she'd had to. The sounds of battle beneath her feet seemed to increase. She heard shouts from Tripp, who was coordinating the attack, as well as a few others she recognized, including Jazz cursing under her breath. None of it was loud enough to hear without the aid of her earpiece.

She'd almost reached the end of the first row she'd been assigned when she heard a gasp from her right, the direction Ty had gone in. Then, the sounds of a struggle broke out all around her as she assumed all three of her teammates were engaged. She hadn't heard any crates opening, anything like that. "Graham?" she whispered, but all she got in response was a grunt that told her he was in trouble.

Determining she needed to go to their aid as quickly as possible, Rachael glanced down the row she was intersecting. Seeing nothing, she broke to her left, went down a few rows, which should've taken her closer to Graham, but she froze about six steps in as a form from the ceiling dropped down in front of her.

Rachael's locket was glowing bright red now. As the figure in front of her stepped forward into the dim light, there was no question who she was standing face to face with.

It was Sasha.

And she was pissed.

KILL HER

Rachael

"WELL, if it isn't just the vampire I've been looking for," Rachael said, not letting the fear that threatened to boil up inside of her erupt. Sasha looked somehow stronger than usual, more fierce. It was enough for the little girl inside of Rachael to want to scream and run the other direction. But she reminded herself she was a grown-ass woman now, the kind that had been trained to kill vampires, and this was one she needed to end sooner rather than later.

Sasha didn't bother to respond to her comment. Instead, she came at Rachael, claws elongated, teeth bared, ready to slice the hunter's face off. Rachael raised her hands and blasted Sasha with her powers. The vampire yelped as the blue light coursed through her, but though it slowed her down, it didn't stop her. Clearly, Sasha had gotten stronger since that day she'd infiltrated Rachael's bedroom and the vampire hunter had been able to freeze her in place while Rex went for help. That wasn't going to work now.

Sasha swiped at her face again, this time connecting, and Rachael felt blood spurt from her cheek bone. She had her gun in her hand

and fired a few quick shots, two of them connecting with Sasha. She squealed at the sting from the silver, but again, she was too strong to be stopped by mere bullets, even if these were especially designed to slow down vampires.

The pain from the cuts on her face was the least of her concern as Sasha recovered from the bullets and came at her again. Jazz wanted her to tether this monster to this place so she could destroy her, but all Rachael wanted to do at the moment was get away from her. As Sasha flung herself at Rachael, the hunter kicked out, connecting with the vampire's gut, knocking her across the space. She hit a stack of crates and knocked them over, landing on her back in a pile of crushed boards.

Rachael drew her silver-tipped spear from the inside of her coat pocket and pounced on top of Sasha, praying she could get the stake inside of her heart before she recovered from her fall.

"Stay down, bitch!" Rachael shouted, working her knees around the outside of the vampire's waist. "I command you to stay in this realm! You're tethered here and cannot leave!"

She hoped some combination of those statements would be enough for Sasha to be tethered the way that Jazz said she should be, but she would have no way of knowing whether or not it worked until Sasha tried to get away.

At the moment, she wasn't trying to leave, but she was trying to get up. She fought against Rachael, whose knees were digging into shards of broken boards, nails, and who knew what else. The pain would have to wait for later. She zapped Sasha with another bolt of blue light, hoping she could subdue her long enough to get the stake in.

Behind her, Rachael heard a hiss and then some sort of angry shriek. She turned to see another vampire coming right at her. Drawing the gun she'd holstered when she pulled the stake, she fired two quick shots, slowing the male vampire, but not destroying him. She raised her hands and sent out a beam of blue light, knocking him back several feet, but Sasha took advantage of the distraction and pushed Rachael off her.

Rachael went flying through the air and crashed into more crates, splintered lumber biting into her back. "Ugh!" The breath was knocked out of her as she struggled to her feet. Sasha was up now, but she wasn't headed toward Rachael. Instead, she and the male vampire who'd just jumped Rachael were running back down the aisle away from her, toward a black circle of light.

"Come on stupid tether, work," Rachael muttered. "You can't leave, Sasha Thornsby!" she shouted.

The vampire kept running, headed for the portal. Rachael stuck out her hands, shooting a stream of blue light at the vampire's back, hoping to grab hold of her and keep her from leaping through the exit.

It didn't matter.

When Sasha reached the portal, her fate was already sealed.

TETHERED

Rachael

RACHAEL WATCHED as Sasha tried to run through the portal and escape, the same way she had the last several times the two of them had combated each other. This time, though, if the tether worked, she shouldn't be able to disappear.

Sasha ran for the black circle of lights, alongside some of her henchmen. When she reached the portal, she collided with what seemed like a brick wall of glass, bouncing back several feet. The other vampires who had scrambled for the exit were able to keep running, but they hesitated just on the other side, not sure if they should come back and aid their leader or get away from the hunters.

"What the hell did you do?" Sasha asked, standing and straightening her clothing as she turned to look at Rachael.

She couldn't believe the tether had actually worked. "You're not going anywhere, Sasha Thornsby," she said through barred teeth.

Sasha glared at her, but then her eyes dropped slightly, and she fixated on the locket around Rachael's neck. It was still glowing a bright red. The closer the vampire came to the hairs Rachael had taken from her on their last encounter, the redder it became. Clearly, Sasha could see the root of her problems. Her eyes never left the locket as she repeated her question with a snarl. "What did you do?"

"What did I do?" Rachael repeated. "It's not what I did--it's what I'm about to do." She raised her hands and began to pool her power, thinking now was as good a time as ever to take Sasha out. The rest of the vampires who were nearby when the portal opened were gone now, having chosen their own asses over helping Sasha, even though Rachael had to assume none of the others were strong enough to open portals themselves, which meant if she destroyed Sasha, none of them would be back....

Rachael shot the ball of blue light at Sasha, and the vampire froze, as she was no longer able to move forward. Her face twisted into a grimace, and her muscles tensed as she did her best to try to fight the power being concentrated on her.

But Rachael was too strong for her. Sasha couldn't move. The vampire continued to do her best to free her feet, to get away from Rachael, but just as she had been stuck that night in Rachael's room, she wasn't going anywhere now.

Unfortunately, Rachael was alone again, as she had been that other time they may have been able to end Sasha if she'd had someone else who was able to move in on the vampire while she couldn't get away. "Graham!" Rachael shouted, praying the one person she had been able to rely on through all of this was somewhere nearby.

She heard nothing in response. It was as if the entire team was gone again, which made no sense since she certainly hadn't followed Sasha into another realm this time. But then, she had somehow managed to set up a barrier to the rest of the world when she was standing in that field as well.

Keeping her hands up, Rachael drew her gun from its holster and emptied the chamber into Sasha. With each bullet, the vampire twitched slightly, but they were not strong enough to kill her, not individually or collectively. It would take a beheading to end Sasha, and Rachael had no idea how she would manage to keep the vampire from moving and still cut her head off.

Despite the bullets, Sasha was beginning to move again, beginning to regain her strength. Rachael needed to end this, and she needed to do it now.

"Son of a bitch," she muttered, deciding there was really only one thing she could do. She'd have to use all of her strength and skills, and even then, there was a chance she would fail. If Sasha knew she was tethered, she might know how to cut the tether, too.

Rachael drew her blade from her jacket pocket, keeping one hand in place so that Sasha was still immobilized. With her knife drawn, Rachael took a deep breath and flung herself at the vampire.

It was impossible to keep Sasha in place and pounce on her at the same time because Rachael couldn't concentrate on both at once. She collided with Sasha, sending her flying backward into a stack of crates, and brought her knife around, catching the vampire in the neck.

Sasha sputtered as blood flowed from her throat, coating her shirt in the thick, red substance. Rachael grabbed her by the shoulders, moving her so that she was flat on the floor, no longer propped up against the crates. She continued to saw at the vampire's neck, spurred on by the possibility that this might all come to an end right now.

Sasha wasn't quitting, though. Even with the growing gash in her neck, Sasha did her best to claw at Rachael's hands, trying to free herself or dislodge the weapon from her hand.

Rachael wasn't playing anymore, though. Months, if not years, of hatred and loathing poured through her as she severed tendons and veins. Once she'd sawed through the vampire's jugular, she stopped moving, and the blood made it hard for Rachael to see what she was doing.

Eventually, Sasha's head came free from her body, and Rachael found herself kneeling in a pool of blood, her pants stained, her hands crimson, panting from the exertion of ending the vampire.

The warehouse around her was still eerily silent as Rachael stood and looked around. "Graham? Jared?" she shouted, but there was no answer. Likewise, there was nothing on her earpiece either. Where was everyone? She had fully expected her team to come back after Sasha was dead because she'd assumed it had been the vampire distorting reality. But now that Sasha was gone, the world didn't come back to Rachael.

Wiping her knife on her pants, she headed for the stairs, praying she'd walk out of whatever it was making it seem like she was all alone, but even when she reached the first floor, she was the only one there.

"What the hell is going on?" Rachael asked, but there was no one there to answer.

STILL NOT GOOD

Rachael

THE BOTTOM FLOOR of the warehouse was desolate. Not a sound filled her ears, other than the sound of Rachael's boots echoing off the concrete floor. She'd been under the impression that, once Sasha died, all of her trickery would come to an end, too. But the fact that she seemed to be in another portal of some sort, sheltered from the rest of her team, made her wonder if she would ever be able to undo what Sasha had done, now that she was dead.

Or was this someone else's work?

Rachael continued to walk, wondering if she went outside if she would have a moment of enlightenment. Or would this strange representation of her own reality continue there as well?

"Hello?" she shouted. "Graham? Jazz?" Would her friends be able to find a way to get her out of wherever the hell she was again?

She had almost reached the exit when she thought she heard footsteps behind her. Rachael froze and turned slowly toward a dark aisle that ran the length of the warehouse. On either side, boxes were stacked nearly to the ceiling, which soared twenty feet over her head.

Someone was walking toward her, slowly, and the cadence of the footsteps sounded familiar.

Rachael took a few steps closer. The shadows still concealed the intruder's identity, but her excellent vision might allow her to penetrate the darkness soon enough, particularly since the figure continued to come closer.

And then, Rachael realized who she was looking at, and her mouth dropped open. Never in a million years had she even considered this a possibility, but here she was, looking into the most familiar face of all of them. This one, however, was different enough to let her know that she hadn't lost her mind and this was either a visitor from another realm or Rachael had been sucked into yet another world. While everything else was exactly as it should be, the person walking toward her had a large set of pointy fangs.

Other than that, she was looking at the same face she'd seen staring back at her from the mirror for as long as she could remember.

"How the hell...."

"I can't believe you're so surprised to see me, Rachael," she said, stopping about ten feet away and folding her arms. "I would've thought you'd have figured out pretty quickly that if there was more than one Chell, and more than one Sasha, there had to be more than one of us."

Rachael sputtered. She was unable to think of anything logical to say. So many questions came to mind. How did this version of her become a vampire? Did she have the same sort of powers that Rachael had? Was she pulling the strings all along? And... was she evil?

As her own eyes narrowed in her direction, Rachael got the idea that she wasn't nice. "What do you want?" she asked the vampire version of herself, trying to be demanding.

"What do you think I want, Rachael? You have something I don't, something I've always wanted. Sasha was supposed to help me, but she got in the way. Probably because she never quite trusted me." She shrugged. "I can't blame her. I turned her into what she was after all."

Rachael remembered the comment Sasha had made in her room,

about how she blamed Rachael for making her. "She thought I made her, when it was obviously you?"

Vampire Rachael shrugged. "She wasn't the brightest bulb, I guess. I mean… she figured it out eventually. But she wasn't strong enough to kill me. I told her if she got the book, she would be able to figure out how to kill you. She got it, and I intended to take it from her, but then she lost it again before I could use it. Your version of our father was much better at this whole scribe thing than mine was. So are you--unfortunately. Therefore, if I want what you have, I'm going to have to take it from you. And take you out of the picture so you don't get in the way."

"How can you do that, exactly?" Rachael asked. "You might be as strong as me, but you're not stronger."

She saw the vampire swallow, which let her know that she was right. "You're in my world now, Rachael. I have more resources here than you do."

Rachael heard movement behind her, outside, in the parking lot. Were those the resources the vampire had mentioned?

She couldn't stand there and wait to find out. Rachael sent a blue ball of power at the vampire version of herself, catching her off guard, and knocking her backward down the row. She careened sideways, flying into a stack of boxes.

No ball of power came back in her direction, which made her think the vampire was bluffing, and she wasn't as strong as Rachael was. "Get up, Dracula!" she shouted, knowing how to push her own buttons. "Come show me how strong you are!"

The vampire was back on her feet, but she had no light to toss in her direction. Rachael could've knocked her down again, but it wouldn't accomplish much. As the noises grew outside, Rachael prepared herself for battle, getting her hands ready, making sure her knife and gun were where she could pull them.

"Do you really think you can beat all of us?" the vampire asked her.

"I guess we'll find out," she replied. She moved away from the door, just in time. Three more vampires walked in.

All of them were people she knew. Again, Rachael was left with her mouth hanging open. Ebony. Frank. Her mom? "Holy hell...." How could she kill those people?

The four vampires rushed her. Rachael didn't have time to think. She drew her gun and began to fire, knocking Frank back a few feet, but the others were strong enough that they kept coming. She kicked out, catching the vampire her in the gut and sending her backward as Ebony's claws bit into her leg and her mother came for her face. "Love you, too, Mom," she muttered, pulling her knife and swinging it at her mom-pire. She dug into the woman's arm, and she staggered backward.

"Rachael!"

That was Jazz's voice. She heard Graham and Jared, too. Taking her eyes off the monsters for a moment, she saw an open portal a few feet away from her. While she would love to stay and finish the fight, she knew she couldn't do this by herself, and none of them were coming to her aid. Maybe they couldn't for some reason?

Rachael blasted the regrouping vampires with a blinding blue light and ran for the portal, diving toward the black circle.

Just as Sasha had been met with a concrete wall she could not see, Rachael smacked into nothing hard enough to knock her on her ass. Why couldn't she get through?

"The locket!" Jazz shouted. "Toss it!"

That made sense. Sasha couldn't get through, so neither could her hair. Rachael grabbed a hold of the locket and yanked it off, tossing it across the room just as the vampires closed in once more. She dove for the portal and watched the bloodsuckers stop on the other side, unwilling or unable to come through.

Panting, Rachael lay on the ground, trying to stop her heart from pounding.

"Are you okay?" Graham asked, kneeling down next to her.

She nodded, but she couldn't form coherent sentences yet.

"Was that... you?" Jared asked.

"Yeah," Rachael muttered. "From another world."

"What the hell?" Sammi asked. "Was she trying to kill you?"

"It sure seemed like it," Rachael muttered, finally able to get her breath back.

"But why?" Marcy asked.

"She said I have something that she doesn't, something she wants."

"What's that?" Graham wanted to know.

Rachael started to say she didn't know, but then she realized she did know after all. "You."

KILLING RACHAEL

Graham

BACK AT THE ACADEMY, Graham lay staring at the ceiling of his bedroom, glad Rachael was able to sleep. They'd been back for a few hours now, and she'd been asleep for most of that time, after a shower and an aggressive cock ride that had let him know she was just as aggravated by what they'd found out that night as he was, if not more so. But she'd worn herself out--either fighting vampires or fucking him--and now she was sound asleep.

He wasn't so lucky, though. Most of the time, he was able to turn off his thoughts and catch a few Zs. But since Rachael had come into his life, things had gotten more complicated, and he'd found it harder to let go of the real world and melt away into a dream state.

How in the world were they going to kill Rachael?

Not the one sleeping next to him, of course, but the vampire version of her. Why hadn't it occurred to any of them that that was what Sasha had meant when she'd accused this Rachael of making her? He'd thought the vampire was talking about the book Rachael had written, but now that he knew what she actually meant, it seemed clear that she couldn't have meant that since she probably didn't even know that this Rachael had written a book.

It still didn't explain how Sasha hadn't realized that the Rachael she was talking to wasn't a vampire, but either she didn't care that it wasn't the exact same one, or maybe she thought she'd gone back in time and not into another dimension.

At least Sasha was dead. That was something, but then, how many other Sashas were there out there in other worlds, waiting to invade this one? As long as none of the scribes started messing with the world again, it shouldn't matter. But vampire Rachael was also a scribe, wasn't she? What kind of damage could she do?

Was there a vampire version of him out there? He didn't think so--at least not one that Vampire Rachael had come across, which explained why she wanted him so badly. It was her plan to turn him into a vampire and claim him. But why in the world would he be incentivized to stay with her if she did that? Could she somehow use her scribe powers to force him to fall in love with her?

Thus the endless questions that were keeping him up at night.

Rachael stirred next to him. He turned and brushed her hair away from her face. She was so beautiful, and she still didn't even know it, even though he told her every day. Where would he be if she hadn't made it into his world? He wasn't sure, but he had the idea he'd still be wallowing in his grief. As much as he'd loved Chell, he hadn't loved her as much as he loved Rachael. If she was still alive, they'd be married by now, and he'd probably be trying to talk her into having children, something they'd never agreed on. He still missed Chell, and he certainly wished all of this could've happened without her dying, but he loved Rachael and knew his life was better with her in it.

He'd have to figure out a way to keep her in it--and keep himself from turning into a vampire. Otherwise, he would be searching for a way to go back in time, and he had an idea that truly was impossible.

He rolled over and closed his eyes, hoping he could find a way to fall asleep. Rachael would probably be up soon, looking for answers, and she wouldn't be able to stop herself from waking him up, one way or another.

Her hair brushed against his back, and he smiled. She draped her arm over his chest, and he pulled her close, thankful she was there with him. She might've written him for herself, but she was perfect for him in every way.

So long as neither one of them was a vampire.

As he started to fall asleep, Graham tried to stay focused on the beautiful naked woman next to him, not her bloodsucking counterpart. If he was going to dream of Rachael, he wanted this version biting his neck, not the one with the fangs....

RACHAEL VERSUS HERSELF

Rachael

RACHAEL SLEPT SO LONG, it was past noon when she woke up. A look
around told her she was alone. She grappled for her phone, hoping
Graham had at least sent her a text to let her know where he'd gone.
"Went to talk to Jared. Hope you feel better when you wake up. Love
you."

She was tempted to put her phone down and go back to sleep, but
thoughts from the night before were playing through her mind again.
She needed to figure out what to do about the sudden appearance of a
vampire version of herself who wanted to kill her and steal her
boyfriend.

What in the world could make her turn out so evil? Sure, she had
her downfalls like everyone, but the version of herself she'd ran into
after she'd killed Sasha was difficult to wrap her mind around.
Nothing she could think of could've possibly made her turn out the
way this other Rachael had. Even though she felt abandoned by her
dad when she was young, never really had a lasting romantic relation-

ship until she was twenty-five and invented one for herself, more or less, and was never very good at school or her job, whatever had happened to Vampire Rachael had to have been really bad.

She remembered seeing other people she cared about turned as well. What had happened to those people? Had Vampire Rachael been the one to turn them, or had it been someone else? Who had turned her?

It was pretty clear that Rachael had been the one to turn Sasha. She wondered if she'd also been the one to turn Chell.

Unfortunately, she wasn't likely to get answers anytime soon. It wasn't as if she could sit down and have a cup of tea with this new version of herself. When they met again, and she could be sure that they would, they'd both be out for blood. There wouldn't be any calling time out and do a quick interview.

Deciding she had too much to do to continue to lie in bed and ask herself questions she had no answer to, Rachael got up and went to take a shower. She'd taken one after she got back from the hunt, but she needed to wake up. When she was done, she sent a text to Graham to figure out where everyone else was. He answered that a few of them had gathered in the staff lounge downstairs to chat.

It wasn't an official meeting or anything, but she was hopeful someone would have some insight into how to handle this situation. She wouldn't mind killing the vampire version of herself, but she had found out that the two Rachaels were fairly evenly matched, which meant it would be hard for either one of them to kill the other.

She walked into the lounge to see Graham, Jared, Sammi, Tripp, and Jazz assembled there. She was a little surprised to see that Jazz was there, but she didn't say anything to the young girl, other than hello.

"We've been trying to come up with a plan to draw vampire Rachael out into the open so we can destroy her," Graham explained as Rachael sat down next to him.

"Have you got anything yet?" she asked, glad that's what they were working on. The sooner they could do just that, and get rid of the woman, the better. She wanted the vampire version of herself dead even more than she'd wanted to destroy Sasha, which was odd considering she shouldn't want to see herself die so badly.

"Not exactly. We feel like she won't wait too long. Now that you know she exists, and her plan with Sasha has fallen apart, she'll likely be quick to strike again," Jared said. He was sitting across the table from her, his chair tilted back so far, Rachael wouldn't be too surprised if he fell backward.

"Okay. So if we think she'll pop up soon, then we probably don't need to figure out how to draw her out. We just need to know what to do to kill her when she reappears," Rachael said with a shrug.

"Maybe, but we still think we better come up with something, just in case she goes radio silent again," Tripp said.

"Yeah, we wanna give her something to come after that she can't refuse, in a scenario that seems pretty perfect. So we need to pick your brain into figuring out how to fool her, how to make her think she's safe when she's not."

"I have no idea," Rachael said with a shrug. "You want me to tell you how to fool myself?"

"Something like that," Graham said. "We might just come up with some possibilities and run them past you. We already know how to get her out into the open. We just don't know how to do it without tipping her off that she's about to be bombarded with fire from every direction."

"I wish we could do that masking thing she does so that I don't know I'm in another world." Rachael shook her head.

"Maybe we can figure that out. If she can do it, maybe you can, too," Jazz said with a shrug.

"I definitely didn't see anything in the book about that, but that doesn't mean it isn't there," Jared said, running a hand through his hair.

"So… we need to figure out how to trick me, how to hide from me, and how to lure me out." Rachael had no idea how they could do all of that.

"I think we know how to lure Vampire Rachael out," Sammi said, her eyes narrowed.

They had mentioned they had a solution to that, Rachael remembered. "How's that?" she asked.

"With me," Graham replied, meeting her eyes.

Rachael swallowed hard--yeah of course. That would do it.

JAZZ EXPLAINS

Rachael

RATHER THAN GOING RIGHT BACK out into the field to try to track down the new threat, Rachael and the rest of the team wanted to take some time to see if they could come up with a foolproof plan to get Vampire Rachael out into the open so they could destroy her in one try to not have to continuously attempt to hunt her down as they had Sasha.

In Rachael's view, the only way to have a chance at that was for one of them to figure out how to disguise the portal openings the way that the vampire had done to her so that she could draw the vampire into another realm and conceal her teammates, as had been done to her more times than she could count at this point.

That would take careful study of the book, though, and even then, she wasn't sure she'd be able to do it. Jazz was reading through the book again to see if she could find it. If the book had re-written itself again, there was a possibility she'd just missed it the first time. She couldn't remember reading anything about it the first time she'd gone through it, and Jazz was pretty detail oriented.

In the meantime, Jared was also looking through some other key texts. He wondered if there was a possibility those books had also been rewritten without him even knowing it.

Rachael, Graham, and Sammi were going to be leading the attack, it had been decided, since Graham would be the bait and it was Rachael that the vampire wanted to destroy. Sammi wanted to help kill Vampire Rachael and also to be there if Vampire Chell was destroyed. If she couldn't do that herself, she at least wanted to witness the demise herself so there'd be no question in her mind that this version of her sister was gone.

Rachael was on her way to go meet with Graham and Jared when Jazz knocked on her door and then pushed her way in, book in hand, not even looking up as she said, "So... I found something. I'm not sure what it says, though."

"What do you mean?"

Jazz blew out a hot breath. "I think it's in the middle of trying to change its damn self or something. It says, 'A portal in disguise can be utilized to shade the discovery of one's enemies by calling upon the sanctified voices of the past.' Like... what the hell?"

Rachael went over what she'd said again and was not any closer to figuring out what it meant the second time she went over it either. "I don't know. Can I see?"

With a shrug, Jazz handed the book over, pointing at a paragraph about halfway down the left side of the page.

What Rachael saw written there wasn't at all what Jazz had just read to her. She looked at her friend and then back at the book. "Use your energy to cloak a portal opening by drawing upon your light and dispersing it slowly, calling upon the air to shift and change around you. Two may work in conjunction to open a portal, one opening, and one masking, but rarely is one entity strong enough to do both at the same time." She looked at Jazz who was staring at her like she was crazy. "That's what it says."

"Say what now?" Jazz came around to stand near her shoulder. " Where the hell does it say that?"

"Right where you pointed," Rachael said, pointing at the paragraph for her.

"No it don't," Jazz insisted. "It says the same damn thing it said when I read it to you."

Shaking her head, Rachael said, "This book is crazy. It says what I told you it says. In other words, if you can open the portal, which clearly you can because you've done it before, I can mask it by using my light and dispersing it slowly, calling upon the air to shift around us, but that's gonna take a lot of practice. I've never tried to do that before."

Jazz was still shaking her head. "Your dad needs to get his shit together. Why can't he just write a damn book that stays the same?"

"I don't know," Rachael admitted, "but we need to go tell Jared and Graham what we found out before it happens again."

"Our luck, it'll shift right before we try to get that bitch to come after Graham," Jazz said, walking with her to the door.

Though Jazz didn't mean to terrify her with the comment, Rachael had to take a few deep breaths and push the idea out of her mind. The fact that something bad could happen to Graham if this operation went wrong was much more terrifying to her than the idea that there was a version of her in the universe that wanted her dead.

"Let's think positive," Rachael insisted.

"That is the positive version of what might happen," Jazz insisted, and it was all Rachael could do to keep from slugging her friend. She wasn't about to ask Jazz what the worst version of what might happen could be because she was certain Jazz would tell her.

TRYING EVERYTHING

Rachael

THE SUN WAS GOING DOWN, which was the only way Rachael could tell that the day was almost over. She'd been out in an open space near the academy since early that morning, doing everything she could to try to attempt to disguise her surroundings so that their plan to trick Vampire Rachael would work. So far, all she'd gotten was some sore muscles, a blister on her foot from the stupid boots she'd chosen to wear, and a whole lotta frustration.

Jazz had come out with her earlier so that they could practice both of their skills at the same time, but after the first two hours, the other hunter had given up saying it was "useless" and headed inside.

Since that time, Rachael had essentially been on her own, though Graham had come out to check on her a few times, and Jared had come by, too. Still, for most of the day, she'd been out there all alone, doing her best to try to get her powers to do what the book said she should be able to do.

She'd been close a couple of times. She'd started to see a shimmering around her and then what looked like white fog rolling in.

However, her arms had grown tired, and the power shifting out of them dulled, before she could pull everything together.

Determined to make this work, Rachael reached down deep within herself, raised her hands, and did her best to concentrate, imagining the power flowing through her, from her core, radiating out into her arms, and leaving her hands in waves. Keeping it slow and steady, she kept her eyes closed and tried to envision the world around her shifting, the landscape morphing from distant trees to mountains and pines. She pictured the fog rolling in, imagined it slowly filling the area around her but staying back so that only the periphery was obscured.

Once she felt her powers ebbing at a steady pace, she opened her eyes. They widened as it looked as if she were making some progress. Twenty feet or so in all directions, a white fog hovered in the air, growing and billowing like clouds as it started to obscure her view, and Rachael thought she saw the beginnings of mountain peaks coming into focus beyond that.

Then, she felt a sputter, as if her magic was beginning to run out again. "No, damn it," she muttered. How had the vampire version of herself been able to do all of this without even keeping her hands up? She'd been able to fight while she kept the world at bay, hadn't she?

Or was that why she hadn't shown up until after Sasha was dead? Was she somewhere else, doing this, while Sasha did her dirty work? If that was the case, then it was no wonder Rachael was struggling with it now. She'd need someone else to kill vampire Rachael if she was busy doing this. Or someone else would have to set up the screen. Was she the only one capable of using her powers this way?

As the lights coming from her hands began to sputter, Rachael felt a wave of defeat wash over her. She might be able to hold it for a few more minutes, but there was no way she could hold it even ten more. They wouldn't have nearly enough time to pull this off under the current conditions.

Frustrated, Rachael pulled her powers back in and collapsed onto her bottom in the middle of the field, covering her hands with her face. "God!" she yelled. Why did this have to be so freaking difficult?

Why couldn't she just summon her power and do whatever the hell she wanted to with it? It looked so easy when the vampires did it!

"Having trouble?"

The sound of a vaguely familiar voice calling out had her eyes open and her hands down, at the ready. Was she too drained to protect herself now, if she needed to?

The scene she'd been summoning was gone now, but the fog lingered. In fact, it had thickened, and then, as a form she'd seen before stepped through the white, she knew why.

Rachael sighed. "Thank goodness," she muttered, pulling herself up off the ground. "Can you help me?"

"I can," her father said, a crooked smile on his face. "But not as much as you can help yourself."

"What do you mean, Dad?" she asked, using a term she never thought she'd be comfortable with as if it was the most natural thing in the world.

"I mean... Rachael, my dear, you're doing it wrong."

LET DAD HELP

Rachael

"What do you mean I'm doing it wrong?" Rachael asked, staring at her dad for only the second time in the last twenty years. After spending the better part of the day attempting to control her powers well enough to disguise a portal opening, she was glad to have the help of someone who clearly knew her own strength better than she did, but his words were more than a little discouraging. "What do I do then?"

"You're trying to pull the power from within you, dear. You need to organize the power around you, pull from the atmosphere, not from yourself. Once you get the energy in order, it will stay in place, and you can do what is necessary to stop the darkness."

"The darkness?"

"The evil version of yourself." His expression seemed to imply he might've been talking about her actual self who had made bad choices.

"Right. Okay. From the atmosphere. No problem." She looked

around, wondering how in the world she pulled energy from nothing. What was around her? Empty air. Grass. The sky.

"There is energy in everything, Rachael. Just because you can't see it doesn't mean it isn't there. You've got to feel it. Call it to you. Then, you can mold it into whatever you'd like for it to be."

"What I want it to be is... invisible. Sort of." She shook her head, not sure how to explain to him what she was trying to do.

Luckily, it wasn't necessary. "I know, Rachael. I know what you're trying to do. You're trying to do this." With a flourish of his hands, her father was able to accomplish what she'd been trying to do all day. The environment around them shifted, a fog lingered in the exterior, but the view in the distance morphed into a deserted beach, complete with crashing waves, and her father stood there, controlling it all without even holding his hands up or breaking a sweat.

"How did you...." Rachael couldn't finish the sentence. It wasn't necessary. "Is there a portal opening nearby, too?"

"Clearly, or else I wouldn't be here. Now, stop making it more difficult than it has to be and feel the power around you, call it to you, and make it do as you wish."

"Easy enough," Rachael said, shaking her head. Her father gave a little wave of his hand and the illusion around them faded away. Now, it was Rachael's turn to try to reproduce exactly what he'd just done.

"Breathe deeply, feel the energy. Harness it."

"Yep, yep," Rachael said, closing her eyes. She did her best to listen and feel out into the world, searching for this stream of energy her father had spoken of. She'd never considered tapping into anything like that before, and if it was as hard as she thought it was going to be, she may as well give up now.

Her father was still talking, but his voice was muffled as Rachael began to feel a tingling sensation all over her body like nothing she'd ever experienced before. Was this the energy he'd been talking about? A visual popped into her mind, and she could see blue lights, similar to the ones that let her know when a portal was opening, dancing in her mind's eye.

Without opening her eyes, she called upon those lights, organizing them with her thoughts, pushing them together. They moved quickly and orderly, just as she commanded them to. It was so odd; she never would've imagined it could be so simple. Soon enough, they were all banded together in a circle of light.

"Now, what do I do with it?" she muttered.

If her father answered her, she didn't hear. Instead, she flipped her hand out, hoping the lights obeyed. In her mind, they moved, and then she envisioned them turning to fog, saw the world beyond them fading away….

Rachael opened her eyes, half believing everything would be as she had last seen it, but when she looked to see if her work had transferred from her mind to reality, she couldn't help but laugh in delight. "It worked!" she exclaimed.

Her father began to clap slowly. "Well done, Rachael. Well done!"

The world beyond the ring of fog was mountainous, the sky an azure blue, just as she'd seen it in her mind. Even when Rachael dropped her hands, nothing changed. She could then use her own power to open the portal or defend herself. Could she also use the energy from the universe to do those things? She wasn't sure, but she hoped so. Perhaps she was more powerful than she even imagined.

"You've done it Rachael. Very well done," Billy said as he came over to her. He wrapped his arms around her, and Rachael rested her head on his shoulder, so very happy to have made him proud. "I love you, daughter."

"Thanks, Dad. I love you, too." A few months ago, she never would've been able to say that, but now she had a better understanding of why he'd been gone.

And she could see that he was leaving again. "I'm sorry. I have to go," he said, as if reading her mind.

Rachael nodded. "Thank you for being here when I needed you most, Dad."

"Just be careful, Rachael. There's no battle more difficult than fighting yourself."

She swallowed hard, wondering if he meant the vampire version of her or literally herself. Either way, he was right. "I'll be careful. You, too."

He laughed. "I'll do my best." He kissed her cheek, and then, he stepped into the fog and was gone.

Rachael called the fog off, and it dissipated, taking the mountains and blue sky with it. Her father was already gone.

But another form was walking toward her from the direction of the academy, and it made her smile to see him coming to her. "You did it!" Graham called.

"I did!" she shouted back. "Did you doubt me?"

"Not for a minute!"

As he reached her, they both started laughing, and then his lips were on hers, and Rachael felt invincible--even against herself.

A PLAN TO KILL HERSELF

Rachael

THE PLAN SEEMED SIMPLE ENOUGH. Rachael and Graham would just spend some time wandering along in the forest, the rest of their team within sprinting distance, trying to draw Vampire Rachael out. While vampire attacks were on the rise nearby, none of the accounts from their network of hunters and associates matched Rachael's descriptions--or Chell's for that matter. So, the team had to assume those attacks were made by other vampires, possibly some working in connection with the new threat. Or maybe it was just a coincidence. While teams in the area continued to hunt those people down, the Silverwood Academy team concentrated on trying to bring down Vampire Rachael and Vampire Chell.

Ordinarily, walking through the woods with Graham would be relaxing. If it wasn't a chilly mid-November, dark night and the woods weren't eerily quiet. Where were the owls and other night birds? Where were the other nocturnal animals? No raccoons or opossums this night? She would've even settled for some spooky bird calls or scratching sounds.

"It's a little too quiet, isn't it?" Graham asked as they continued to wind their way through the dark trees, his grip on her hand increasing.

"I know. I was just thinking the same thing. Do you think it's because we're out here--or something else?"

"I don't know," he admitted, "but I've spent a lot of time in the woods at night and have never had this happen before."

Rachael couldn't say the same. The only time she'd spent wandering at night in the dark forest was looking for vampires, and since most of the time she'd been working with the team from Silverwood had been in the city, she didn't have a whole lot of experience with that either.

The trees in front of them narrowed so that Rachael had to go in front of Graham to get through. She carefully stepped over exposed roots, watching the piles of leaves to make sure she didn't trip, and walked into a clearing. A noise to her left caught her attention. She whirled around, her hands ready in case it was an assailant.

A large bird with black feathers flew out of a nearby tree, cawing, as it shot off across the starlit sky. Her heart pounding out of her chest, Rachael dropped her hands. "God, it was just a bird."

She fully expected Graham to say something, like, "Yeah, it scared me, too," but when she turned back around, he was gone.

"Graham? Graham?" she called, turning back to the spot where she'd come through the trees. He wasn't there. She spun around frantically. He wasn't anywhere. "Graham!"

"What's going on?" she heard Jared's voice in her ear and was thankful she didn't seem to be completely alone. Maybe Graham had just stepped through the clearing a different way? No, that didn't make sense.

"I can't find Graham," she said. Knowing they were following the pair on video, she hoped they'd seen which way he'd gone. "Do you know where he's at?"

"He's with you," Jared said, confusion marring his voice. "I can see both of you, holding hands on the video feed."

"What? No, he's not. I'm standing in a clearing by myself. I let go of his hand to go between the trees." She looked up and noted a full moon above her, something she hadn't noticed before. "Where the hell am I?" she asked. Had she gone through a portal herself?

Rachael went back the way she came. "Jared, you need to let him know that's not me."

"How do I know you're you?" he asked, his voice a little more snarky than usual. "Maybe he's with Rachael and you're Vampire Rachael."

"Don't be ridiculous!" Rachael shot back. "Jared! Tell him that's not me!"

"If you're you, you can tell him yourself!" Jared shouted back, and then Rachael realized it didn't make sense that she could communicate with Jared but not Graham, if everything was okay with the team's tech. If Jared could hear her, and he could see Graham, she should be able to communicate with Graham.

Unless it wasn't Jared she was talking to….

"Shit," Rachael muttered. She saw nothing back the way she'd come except for darkness and trees. How had the vampires managed to lure them into a trap when they'd been the ones trying to lure the bloodsuckers out? None of this made any sense!

She turned around and ran back into the clearing. The moon was bright enough to light the spaces between the first row of trees, spaces that were slowly beginning to fill in… with billowing clouds of white fog.

"Rachael!" she shouted at the top of her lungs. "What have you done with him?"

The woods were no longer silent. Instead, she heard the echoes of laughter all around her. It was familiar enough to know that it was her own voice, though demented in a way she hoped she never sounded. "Rachael!" she shouted again.

A form appeared between two of the trees, walking through the fog. It wasn't Rachael though, and she could tell by the way that he was walking that it wasn't exactly the person she'd lost either. It was definitely Graham, though. Rachael held her breath, afraid to discover what might've happened to him.

With her heart pounding in her chest, Rachael stepped forward, praying that she hadn't lost him forever.

THAT'S NOT HER

Graham

"Rachael?" Graham called, not sure where she'd gone to. He thought she'd stepped between the trees in front of him, but he'd lost track of her for a second in the darkness, and when he followed her through, she was no longer there. "Rach?"

"I'm right here," she said, walking through a thin veil of fog off to the side in the clearing. "Did you see something weird? Did it get darker for a few seconds?" she asked, looking around at the tops of the trees.

"No." He glanced up, too, but didn't see anything now. He was more concerned with his girlfriend. Something seemed a little off.

"Huh. Weird. I couldn't see you for a minute," she said with a shrug and then reached for his hand. "Where the hell is that stupid Rachael anyway?"

"You mean… the other one?" he asked, her fingers slipping into his. Her hand felt colder than usual.

"Of course. Obviously, I'm right here."

"Obviously." They continued to walk, but the uneasy feeling

Graham had felt when he stepped through the clearing and saw her standing there didn't fade away. Was it possible that Vampire Rachael had somehow snuck in between them and taken his Rachael's place? That might explain her cold hands and the strange behavior. It would certainly explain the odd feeling he had in his stomach.

"Is everything okay, babe?" Rachael asked as they continued on their way. The trees looked similar everywhere Graham looked, as if they were walking in a circle.

"I guess so. Just… tired," he said.

"You? Tired? When are you ever tired?"

She had him there. He wasn't tired very often. "Tired of walking around in the woods," he said.

She nodded. "Me, too. Maybe we should call it a night."

"Maybe just a little while longer." He certainly wasn't taking this Rachael back home with him, not until he knew for sure she was the right one.

"Graham, are you okay?" Jared asked in his ear.

His eyes immediately went to Rachael. Had Jared been talking to her, too? Or was this directly to him. "Hold on a second, Rach," he said, letting go of her hand. She looked at him with her eyebrows knit as he stepped away. "Not sure," he said to Jared. "Why?"

She wasn't about to let him have a private conversation with anyone. She looked confused. Rachael closed the distance and stopped in front of him, her arms folded.

"Well, I can see you on the video with Rachael, but she just asked me where you are."

"Who are you talking to?" Rachael asked, staring at him.

Graham swallowed hard. "You mean, you can't hear that?" he asked.

"I'm only talking to you," Jared confirmed. "Should we be concerned?"

"Hear what? Are you feeling all right, Graham?" Rachael asked him. Then, her eyes widened slightly, and she said, "Oh, you mean the other team members? Are you talking to them? I forgot about them."

She let out a nervous giggle. "I was thinking it was just you and me walking around out here."

Not wanting to tip her off just yet that he'd figured out she was not who she claimed to be, he laughed. "Silly. Yeah, I was just talking to the guys back at the academy."

She nodded, but he wasn't completely sure she believed his lie either.

"So… that's not the real Rachael?" Jared asked.

Graham shook his head, knowing Jared could see him because he'd just said he could.

"Shit," Jared mumbled. "How did that happen?"

Graham shrugged but then started walking next to the fake Rachael again. At the moment, he didn't care how it had happened, he just needed to get rid of this Rachael and find his girlfriend--before something catastrophic happened.

"We're coming in now, Graham," Jared said.

He gave a slight nod, but he could tell by the body language of the creature next to him that she was no longer under the illusion that Graham was fooled. It wouldn't be long until she turned on him. He just hoped his team was there in time to help him out or she wasn't as powerful as she had appeared the last time he saw her in action. If she was even half as powerful as his Rachael, Graham was in trouble.

ALONE IN THE WOODS

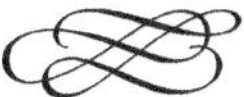

Rachael

"GRAHAM, WHERE WERE YOU?" Rachael asked, watching the form come through the fog. Even though he looked like the man she loved, she was certain this wasn't him coming toward her. It wouldn't make sense that Jared said he saw Graham holding her hand, yet he was standing in front of her. Either that or something had happened to Jared. The fact that she couldn't hear him at all now made her think that she had somehow managed to walk right into one of Vampire Rachael's traps.

"I was just… over there," he said, his voice sounding off in a way Rachael couldn't put her finger on.

Never one to beat around the bush, she pulled her gun. "Stop," she said. "I'm not an idiot. Who are you really?"

"What do you mean?" She could see his lavender eyes now, even though it was dark. They seemed to be glowing in the faint light from the heavens.

"Don't even try to convince me you're Graham. I know you're not. Who are you?"

"Rachael, baby, it's me."

Rather than shooting the creature in front of her, Rachael decided to use her newfound powers to see if they were capable of revealing the truth. She put her gun back inside of her holster and summoned the energy around them to disperse any other energy that might be at use.

Nothing happened, nothing but a slight stirring in the fog surrounding them. Did that mean that someone else had already summoned all of the energy here, had already put it to use?

He continued toward her, the look on his face not the friendly smile she was used to. "What are you doing, Rachael?"

"Getting away from you," she said, not sure what she was battling. She took two giant strides backward, into the fog, and through it to the darkness of the trees, assuming he would follow.

But he didn't. Not that she could detect anyway. Rachael's eyes searched the darkness, digging through the trees, searching for him. Was she outside of the portal now? Would she be able to pull together the energy from the forest?

"Rachael?" The voice so similar to Graham's called out from somewhere in the trees, but she couldn't pinpoint where he was. "Oh, Rachael?"

She spun around, searching for any indication of where he might've gone. "Reveal yourself!" she insisted.

The sing-song voice met her ears again--from behind her, in front of her, everywhere.

Refusing to play the victim, Rachael summoned the energy again. This time, a blue glow filled her hands. She quickly pushed it out around her, illuminating the dark spaces between the gnarled tree trunks.

Turning around again, she searched for him, lighting up the area between the trees. Where was the real Graham? Why wasn't Jared's voice filling her head if she had stepped out of the portal? And where the hell was this shapeshifting vampire?

From out of nowhere, he dropped down in front of her, maybe out of a tree. Rachael jumped back as Graham's voice chuckled. "There she is," he said in a whisper that sent chills down her spine. "There's my girl."

Rachael pulled her energy together to hit him in the chest with a beam of the blue light. It didn't change his form, but it was enough for him to stop walking. Pain radiated from his chest, down his limbs, his head tipping back as his eyes rolled into the back of his head and his arms and legs shook. She did her best to increase the bolt of energy coursing through him, wondering how much more it would take for him to explode when she heard another somewhat familiar voice from the darkness off to her left.

"Stop! You're killing him!"

She turned her head to see Chell there, the vampire version, the look of misery on her face conveying that she felt awful for the vampire in front of her.

"That's sort of the point, Chell," Rachael said, returning her attention to the vibrating man in front of her.

"But it's not our fault!" she protested, coming over. "Please, Rachael! Let him go! I can't lose him again!"

"Again?" she asked. Confusion washed over her as she tried to piece together what was happening. Was this an alternate reality version of Graham?

"Rachael, I'm not powerful enough to defeat you, so I'm begging you to let him go, let us explain. Please."

For some reason she couldn't quite understand, Rachael felt sorry for the vampire girl standing next to the bloodsucker vibrating with enough power he looked like he might succumb at any moment.

"I better not regret this," Rachael said as she lowered her hands. The version of Graham before her toppled backward into Chell's arms. Rachael didn't lower her hands. She might feel bad for these two, but she wasn't an idiot. Was she?

DOUBLES

Rachael

"YOU'D BETTER START EXPLAINING," Rachael said, glaring at Vampire Chell, who lowered Vampire Graham to the ground next to her. He still looked a little dazed, but Rachael had faith he'd come around in a few minutes. It wasn't as if she'd attempted to explode his head or anything. That gorgeous head would be a terrible thing to waste, even if it did come with pointy teeth.

"We aren't from here--I mean your world. I think you know that already," Chell began.

"I know you're not the same Chell that died a month before I arrived at Silverwood. But you must know, that's not my world either, not exactly," Rachael said, resting her hands on her hips. Chell alternated between looking at her Graham and Rachael.

"I guess so. I mean, I'm not exactly sure about all of that. All I know is, a vampire version of you showed up in our world a few months ago. She was hellbent on taking Graham back here with her. Of course, I didn't want to let him go, and he didn't want to go either,

"

but she threatened to destroy him if he didn't consent, and she seemed powerful enough to do it."

"So… she brought me to what I assumed was her world," vampire Graham said, getting his strength back enough to talk. "She locked me in a room in an old house, trying to coax me into falling in love with her, which I didn't do, for obvious reasons."

Trying not to be offended herself, Rachael had to assume his response had more to do with kidnapping than her looks.

"Eventually, I was able to get through, too, but it was hard, and I brought some nasty people with me."

"Like Sasha?" Rachael asked, wrinkling her forehead as she tried to figure all of this out.

"Yes. She was convinced that Rachael had turned her, so she wanted to hunt her down. I didn't bother to try to tell her that wasn't the same Rachael we knew from before. It's all so complicated when you're talking about multiple versions of yourself." Chell ran a hand through her blonde hair.

"You're telling me," Rachael nodded. "Did a version of me turn you?"

"No. But a version of you did turn Sasha--my friend Sasha. I think when the other Sasha came through, some of the worlds got mingled together and changed the reality here. Is that possible?"

"Hell, at this point, anything and everything is possible." Rachael tried to stay with Chell as she continued to explain.

"So… I followed Graham through, bringing some version of Sasha with me. She went after you, thinking you were the Rachael she wanted to kill--but honestly, it wasn't even this Vampire Rachael she wants. At least, I don't think it is."

"It could be," Rachael said with a shrug. "I'm hopeful there aren't too many vampire versions of me out there."

Chell shook her head. "Anyway, you killed her, and I was able to find my Graham, and I just about had him free when vampire Rachael decided to try a different version of Graham--your version. I promised we'd help her if she'd let us go when she was done with this trick, the one we're in the middle of right now."

"But you're helping me instead?" Rachael asked.

"Yeah. You seem to be the lesser of the two evils," Vampire Graham said, standing up.

"I'm not evil at all," Rachael replied, glaring at him.

He shrugged. "I'm not willing to accept that until Chell and I are back in our own world."

"It's different there," Chell said. "The majority of people are vampires, but we're not dangerous. We have other methods of sustaining ourselves that don't require us to kill humans."

"Wow--I'd love to hear about that," Rachael said, thinking that might be a game changer for her current world situation. "I mean, not now. Obviously."

"Right. We need to get to your Graham before it's too late," Chell said with a nod. "She's not trying to take your boyfriend hostage the way she kidnapped mine."

Rachael swallowed hard, not even wanting to ask the question since she had a feeling she already knew the answer. Yet, she asked it anyway. "What is she planning to do with him?"

"The vampire version of you wants to turn him into what she is--a vampire," Graham said. "Trust me--being human is better."

Rachael agreed with him. "Then… lead the way." She gestured with her arm, praying they knew where to go. If Vampire Rachael managed to sink her teeth into her Graham before she could get there, and she started the process by which he'd be transformed into a vampire, Rachael's only choices would be to force him to move on to another world, one like the one Chell just described, where vampires were not the enemy. Or destroy him. Seeing as though Chell's world already had a Graham, that wouldn't bode well for her man. She needed to get to him. Now.

DOES SHE BELIEVE ME?

Graham

"You know, you're right. Maybe we should call it a night," Graham said, holding the stranger version of Rachael's hand like it was the rotting carcass of a dead rodent, full of maggots that might explode at any second.

"Okay. Are you going to tell our friends through your little ear thingy, or shall I?"

"They can see us," Graham said, wondering how it was that this Rachael suddenly remembered or realized that they weren't the only one in the woods. Or was she just trying to get more information from him?

"Right, but, will they know where we are going?"

"They can hear us."

She shook her head like she should've known that. "That's right."

"Rachael, are you okay?"

"Yeah, yeah. I'm fine. I'm just a little tired."

"Okay. Well, as soon as we get back to the academy, you can go to bed."

"Yeah," she said again, but Graham could tell there was something else going on. She wasn't tired, and she wasn't just uninterested in what he had to say. She was up to something.

He hadn't been out in the field with his own Rachael when she'd been drawing upon the energy in the air around them, but he'd seen her do it a time or two from afar, and now, seeing the look on this Rachael's face, he realized that's what she was doing now. While he wouldn't know for sure what her purpose was until it was too late, he didn't intend to let it get that far either.

"Rachael!" he said, jumping away from her and simultaneously blasting her with a wave of power from his own hands. He knew his powers were nothing compared to hers, but she didn't see them coming. The bolt of energy was enough to zap her several feet away from him.

"What the hell!" she shouted, hitting the ground hard. He saw a ball of light in her palm as she reached out to steady herself, but it dissipated as she placed her hand on the ground to push up to standing. "What's the matter with you, Graham?"

"Come on. You can't seriously think you could fool me indefinitely, did you? I know you're the vampire version of my girlfriend. I know you somehow managed to separate us, and that you're here to either turn me or take me hostage to get her."

"You've lost your mind!" she said, standing and showing him her teeth. "Do you see any fangs?"

"I don't have to see fangs to know what I'm dealing with! I know how it works. I've been fighting vampires my entire life, Rachael. I don't even want to call you that. You're nothing like my Rachael. She would never try to steal someone else's man away from her."

"Isn't that exactly what she did?" the vampire asked, her eyes widening as she admitted she wasn't exactly who she was supposed to be. "Didn't she kill Chell in your world so she could come here and have you?"

"No! A vampire killed Chell. Rachael had nothing to do with that."

She laughed, her hands beginning to circle again. She was trying to keep him distracted away from what she was really doing so that she could pull together that rush of energy she'd need to disable him long enough to snag him or bite him. "You can't really think that's true. You're not that stupid are you, Graham?"

He pulled his gun. The last thing he was going to do was argue with a vampire about his girlfriend. As he pulled the trigger, she raised her hand, sending a surge of blue light his direction. Graham went flying backward into the trees. It wasn't the full charge, not the kind he'd seen his Rachael use before, but it was enough to make his entire body go numb--except for his head which slammed against the trunk of a tree. He felt blood trickling down the back of it as his vision went blurry. Despite his best efforts, she'd been too strong for him to take on by himself. Now, as the world started to go fuzzy, he saw her walking his direction, her pace slow as if she were about to pounce on him.

Graham had lost his gun when he went flying into the trees, so he mustered all of his strength and sent a beam of light in her direction, but it did next to nothing. He was too weak at the moment to even defeat himself. "Jared! Where are you?" He felt like he was shouting, but the sound of his voice was foreign to him, it was so weak.

"We're almost there!" Jared said. "Just hold on a few more seconds."

"I don't have a few more seconds," Graham replied, his voice fading as the vampire came even closer. His pithy attempt at delaying her had done nothing.

There was no doubt this woman was not his Rachael as she hovered over him, her fangs on full display in what little moonlight could filter through the branches of the tree he was lying against.

"Don't… do it…." he said, not wanting to beg but also not wanting to become a vampire. If she were to infect him, he'd have to be destroyed. In their version of reality, vampires weren't allowed to live, even if they were "good." Not that he'd want to live that way anyway. Perhaps there was another version of reality where he would be safe to live as a vampire, but he doubted his teammates would be willing to hold onto him long enough to help him find his way to that land. No, if she turned him, he was as good as dead.

Rachael dropped down on her knees, running her hand across his cheek. Graham tried to summon enough strength to push her off, but he was losing a lot of blood, and he couldn't get himself to even sit up, let alone defeat her. When she'd tossed him, she'd done it hard. Maybe he'd get lucky and die before she bit him.

A hiss parted her red lips even wider as she leaned in close to him, pushing his head to the side with one hand so she could easily access his neck. Graham pushed up against her, doing his best to force her back. He accomplished nothing. As she lowered her head to his neck, he closed his eyes, bracing himself for the piercing sting of fangs meeting vein.

HE'S DYING

Rachael

VOICES FILTERED through the trees in front of her as Rachael picked up speed, running along with two vampires she probably shouldn't trust, but she truly had no choice at the moment as they pointed her toward the place where she'd come through the portal. It didn't seem as if she were too far from Graham's current location, but it would take her a minute or two to reach him. Branches reached out and clawed her face, ripping at her clothes, threatening to trip her as she cut between them.

In a clearing, two forms came into view, and she realized she was looking at a different version of herself, staring down her boyfriend. Then, an exchange of power, some flying bullets, and Graham hitting a tree trunk hard made Rachael realize she was running out of time.

As Vampire Rachael closed in on him, motion caught her attention on the other side of the tree, and the true Rachael saw her teammates coming in from the other direction. They weren't going to make it to Graham's aid in time, though. The vampire's fangs caught the moonlight as she lowered her head toward Graham's neck, her hand pushing his chin out of the way, her teeth ready to sink into the warm flesh just over his major artery so that she could end the man Rachael knew and loved, turning him into a monster.

She couldn't allow that to happen.

Remembering the lesson her father had taught her, Rachael gathered as much power as she could from the surrounding environment and hastily melded it together. As the vampire version of herself lowered her head, she sent a beam of light arching in her direction, praying it was enough to knock her off kilter until the rest of the team could help.

The beam of light hit the vampire in the back, causing her to sit up abruptly, her back arching the other direction, her sharp teeth pointed up in the air. Graham still wasn't moving, which was alarming by itself, but at least he wasn't at the mercy of the monster now as Jared and Tripp both began to unload their weapons in Vampire Rachael's direction.

The vampire hissed in anger at the rest of the team. She wasn't hurt from the beam of light. Rachael hadn't had the time to gather enough power to injure her, but she had bought Graham more time.

With the other hunters coming in from the other direction, vampire Rachael's choices were limited. Rather than attempting to fight back or even deflect their bullets, she gathered what power she could together and opened up a new portal to her left. Rachael wanted to breathe a sigh of relief. Even though vampire Rachael would still be out there, at least she wouldn't have Graham.

Or would she?

The portal was open, Vampire Rachael was moving toward it, but she wasn't going alone. The bloodsucker looped her hand underneath Graham's shoulder and lifted him off the ground, using her strength as a vampire and the energy flowing around her to pick him up like he was a child.

"Graham! No!" Rachael shouted, praying he found enough energy to fight her off, to do whatever he could to keep from going with her. If she got him through the portal, she'd turn him immediately, which meant they were only delaying the disaster by stopping her from biting him here.

Vampire Rachael lunged toward the swirling lights of the portal, Graham coming along with her, his head tipped to the side in such a way that made Rachael wonder if he was even conscious. Her teammates could no longer shoot their guns because they might hit Graham, but Rachael had to try again. She came to a skidding stop, her hands up as she did her best to summon the energy from the forest, pulling the power away from the vampire and toward her, preparing to send it back her direction in a surge that should put her at a standstill.

But it wasn't working fast enough, and as Rachael disappeared through the portal, Graham was half in and half out. What was she to do?

The two vampires who had been running next to her didn't stop. In fact, they somehow managed to speed up. Both Chell and Vampire Graham were sprinting toward the portal. Rachael watched them in horror, wishing she'd destroyed them when she had a chance. They hadn't helped her at all! This had all been part of Vampire Rachael's plan to take Graham from her.

Out of options, Rachael sent the blast of power she'd pulled together through the portal at Vampire Rachael, praying it would be enough for her to drop Graham outside of the portal so that someone could grab him and pull him to safety.

This beam of power was larger. Blue light sizzled and popped as the ball of light flew across the woods, splitting between the two blurry vampires and landing directly on target, hitting Vampire Rachael squarely in the back.

Not giving her any time to recover, Rachael did her best to redirect her power and latch onto Graham in an attempt to pull him back, but it wasn't working the way she hoped, and she couldn't see him moving at all.

Vampire Rachael was still screaming from the pain of the last blow, but she was far enough into the portal now that she couldn't be seen. The lights appeared to be closing, and Graham was so close to being sucked away from her forever. The two running vampires were close enough to dive in themselves, then the four of them would disappear beyond the portal's edge. Even if Rachael were able to hunt her Graham down, he'd never be the same.

Her options were fading. She was running out of time, power, and patience. What else could she possibly do to keep Rachael from taking Graham away from her forever?

The portal was closing, the vampires were diving, time was standing still, and the world seemed to be coming to an end.

Would she have to say goodbye to the man she loved forever?

THIS ENDS NOW

Graham

GRAHAM WAS HALF IN and half out of the portal. Struggling against the pain, he attempted to gather enough strength to dive back for the opening, Vampire Rachael's claws digging into his shoulder. He saw his own face headed in his direction at a sprint, as well as Chell, and while it was tempting to think this might be his fiancée, the woman he had loved and intended to marry, he had to remind himself that she was a vampire and not to be trusted.

Until she reached his location, and he realized, she was attempting to help. As the other version of himself flung himself at Vampire Rachael, knocking her off balance, her hand springing free from its grip on his shoulder as the large male inflicted pain in the same location that his Rachael had hit her with a beam of light.

Chell had him now, but she wasn't trying to force him into the closing portal. She was sending him back the other direction. "What... why are you helping?" he stammered, wishing he had enough strength to say more.

She didn't answer, only pushed him out through the closing hole.

He thought he saw tears in her eyes, but there wasn't time to register much of a reaction, emotional or otherwise, as she had to turn her attention to vampire Rachael who was gearing up to launch her own attack against the couple.

As Graham fell through the portal opening, tumbling toward the ground, time seemed to stand still for a long moment as he was able to ponder how ironic it seemed that somewhere out there in the universe, a version of him was with the woman he'd loved first, the woman he thought he'd spend eternity with, that even though it wasn't quite the same since they were both the same sort of creatures he and his Chell had spent years hunting and destroying, it was still a fact that an alternate Graham and an alternate Chell were in love and would be together forever, assuming Vampire Rachael wasn't able to destroy them.

The portal was closing, and his last glimpse of Chell faded away. He fully expected to hit the ground, but instead found himself float-ing, and the face looking down at his was similar to the monster that had just done her best to drag him through the hole in the forest wall, but it wasn't that evil creature at all.

A smile took over his face as he looked into Rachael's eyes. He could see the relief as the muscles around her lips softened and her eyes took on the sparkle she reserved for him. Gently, Graham was lowered to the ground, and he felt his energy coming back to him as she brushed her hand across his cheek. "How are you?" Rachael--his Rachael--asked.

"I'm okay," he assured her. "I just need a minute to catch my breath."

She leaned down and kissed his forehead, the shuffling of foot-steps behind him letting him know that the others had arrived as well. All too little too late, save the vampires who'd been the ones to keep him safe, though the surge of power from Rachael's hand should be leaving a sting for a while on her vampire counterpart.

Graham was ready to go home, to give up the fight for one night, regroup, and come back some other time. His team had other plans, though. Over Rachael's shoulder, he saw Jazz, her hands extended, and realized she was doing her best to reopen the portal the vampires had just gone through. "What is she doing?" he asked, managing to scramble up to sitting.

"Going after them," Rachael said. There was a hesitancy in her voice that told him she wasn't as confident that this was a good plan as the others.

Jared addressed both of them. "If we can track them down, now is the time to end this. Otherwise, it will just keep going. Forever."

Rachael stood, turning to face him. "We have to help Chell and the other Graham get back to their own world, though. They were brought here against their will, and if it hadn't been for their help, Graham would be gone now." She looked around the crowd, addressing the rest of the team. "We can't hurt them. Is that clear to everyone?"

Most of the team nodded, but Jared's eyes narrowed. "If they get in the way, we'll do what has to be done."

Rachael glared at him. "Then… don't let them get in your way."

Realizing it was up to him to settle this, Graham pulled himself to standing, grunting against the pain and the wave of nausea that washed over him. "They helped me. We'll help them, too," he said, starting with his eyes glued to Jared's but then moving to the others. He looked at each individual member of his team and made sure that they were all on the same page before he looked at Rachael and nodded.

She gave him a thankful smile, and then Graham realized there was a soft glow beginning to form behind her head. He shifted his eyes to see Jazz had a portal open. Was it the right one? How would they know?

"I think I've got it!" Her confidence was enough to invigorate all of them.

"How do you know for sure?" he asked, the pain subsiding as he stepped closer to her.

"I don't know for sure," she said, "but it looks the same. It feels the same."

"Are you sure you can get us back?" Tripp asked her.

Jazz shook her head. "There are no guarantees in this life, but I think I probably can. Eventually."

"Great. That makes me want to run through," Sammi said under her breath.

Graham was right there with her, but he also wanted this over. "I have faith in Jazz's ability to get us back. If we want to end this, then let's get on with it," he said, seeing most of his team nod in agreement. A few of them stood perfectly still, like they were too scared to move.

"All right then," Jared said, stepping to the front of the group. "Let's get this over with." Jared stepped through the portal and kept walking, giving the rest of the team no choice but to follow. Graham took a deep breath, took Rachael's hand, and stepped through, hoping this was the right place, and they could end Vampire Rachael once and for all.

THE CHASE CONTINUES

Rachael

JAZZ HAD THE PORTAL OPEN. Peering through the opening, it seemed to Rachael that she had gotten it right, and this was the location Vampire Rachael had just disappeared through, taking Chell and the alternate Graham with her. She'd promised them she'd help them get home, and they'd definitely come through with their end of the bargain, helping Rachael get her Graham back. If it hadn't been for the two of them, Vampire Rachael would've disappeared through the opening with her Graham in tow, and he wouldn't be human anymore.

"All right, we'll do our best to help those two, " Jared said behind her, "but finding Vampire Rachael and putting an end to this has to be our top priority."

Rachael glared at her friend over her shoulder. She wasn't exactly sure what had gotten into him. It wasn't like Jared to make such declarations, like he was suddenly in charge. Had the fact that Graham had been temporarily out of commission made him think he was the leader now? Or had the world shifted again with the opening of new portals and actually put Jared in charge?

That theory was shot down when Graham said, "Jared, thank you for handling the situation when I was laid out, but I'm fine now. If Rachael says we need to help the two that just saved my life, then I'm with her on that one. Let's just get through the portal and see what we're facing. We'll go from there."

It seemed clear that the professor wanted to argue, but he only nodded. Graham didn't hesitate to step through the portal, so Rachael went with him, praying Jazz would know how to get them back.

Not the entire team came through. Whether Graham had given an order she missed, or they'd just decided not to, she couldn't tell. Was it possible the portal closed before everyone who wanted to come made it through? Surely not. But when the blue lights stopped dancing and the black smoke cleared, Rachael found herself standing in a forest eerily similar to what she was used to--with Jazz, Graham, Jared, Sammi, Tripp, Marcy, and Flint. Whether or not this team was strong enough to do what needed to be done with no other help was hard for her to say. She just had to assume they were. And hope that her powers were as strong here as they were in the world she was used to.

The sound of a strange bird calling through the darkness made her jump. It was a mix between an owl and a mourning dove, haunting but also some sort of warning. It sent a chill up her spine.

"Where did they go?" Jazz asked, her voice just a whisper. "It didn't take me that long to find the same damn world."

"Good question," Sammi replied as she took a few steps closer, in between the trees. "Maybe this place just looks like where they disappeared."

"No way; this is the same place." Jazz was clearly irritated that Sammi would accuse her of taking them all to the wrong location.

They spread out slightly, though Rachael could tell everyone was leery of taking their eyes off the rest of the party. She had Graham's hand, and there was no way she was going to let go of it this time, not until she absolutely needed both hands so that she could use her powers to end that awful version of herself who'd been causing so much chaos the last several months.

After a few minutes of searching, none of them were able to come up with anything. "I think we need to come back together and come up with a plan," Graham said through the earpiece. Rachael was glad she could hear him through it now. Before, when Vampire Rachael was messing with her, she hadn't been able to hear him at all, and she assumed he couldn't hear her either, or else he would've known from the very start the woman holding his hand wasn't his girlfriend.

Once they were all back in the same vicinity, Graham said, "I really don't want to split up, but I don't see any alternative. This world might look like the one we are used to, but for all we know, we are the bad guys here. This could be a world full of vampires that hunt us. So we've got to be careful. Don't approach anyone except for the three we are looking for. Always stay within view of at least one other teammate, and stay within radio range as well. We can't stay here too long. Pair up, and we'll figure out which directions we'll go."

It just took a moment for everyone to grab a partner. Rachael didn't want to be too far away from Jazz since she was the most likely to get them home, but Jazz was with Jared. Tripp and Sammi were together, and of course Marcy and Flint, who always worked together. There was no question she would be with Graham.

He quickly assigned them general areas to explore. "I want to hear your voices on the radio every five minutes. I'll let you know when I think we need to come back, but if you lose track of me, just come back to this spot, and Jazz will get you home." He caught the young girl's eyes, and she nodded with a confidence beyond her years.

The rest of the team headed off in their directions, and she and Graham turned to face the dark forest together--again. With any luck, they'd have more success this time than they had the time before.

"Do you think this is going to work?" Rachael asked after several minutes of walking along in silence, her gun drawn and in her free hand.

"I sure hope so. I was hoping this was Vampire Rachael's home world, and she'd be willing to stick around here for a while, but I can't imagine she would've taken off that fast."

A thick white fog began to roll between the trees close to the ground, causing a sheen of perspiration to bead up on Rachael's upper lip and her hairline. She recognized that fog. Vampire Rachael seemed to be messing with them again. Could they unknowingly walk through another portal opening and become separated not only from the rest of the team but from her world, possibly indefinitely if Jazz couldn't find them and Rachael couldn't figure out how to get home again. The feeling of panic began to bubble up inside of her.

"Are you okay?" Graham asked, likely feeling her palm become sweaty.

"Yeah, I'm fine," she lied, not wanting to tell him the truth, that she was about to have a panic attack.

"Are you sure because--" Before he could finish, an ear piercing scream split the night sky. They both jumped and turned in the direction from which the wail had come. It didn't sound like anyone's voice Rachael recognized, but when she looked at Graham's face, she could tell he wasn't thinking the same thing.

"Was that...?"

"Chell," he said with a nod. "Come on. Maybe we can help her this time."

Rachael nodded, but when he let go of her hand to tear between the trees, she couldn't help but think of it as if he were running to his former fiancée, not a vampire who happened to look like her. Pushing down her jealousy, Rachael followed behind, hoping they were able to help the woman who had helped them, even if she did have the same face as the woman whose death had gotten her into all this trouble in the first place.

CHELL IS DYING AGAIN

Rachael

FOLLOWING Graham as he sprinted through the foliage, hampered by the dark and the same fog that had preceded every attack by Vampire Rachael since they'd realized the woman existed, Rachael's heart was banging in her chest, not just because of the adrenaline rush and the cardio work out she was getting but because she wasn't sure why Graham was in such a hurry to reach the bloodsucking version of his dead fiancée. She knew it was silly of her to think Graham might have feelings for the vampire. She was already with an alternate version of Graham himself, after all, but was it possible the reason he was running so quickly toward the sound of her screaming now was because he was still hung up on his dead lover?

Deciding now probably wasn't the best time to dissect their relationship, Rachael focused her attention on where they were headed, hoping not to trip over a protruding root or a large fallen branch obscured by a pile of leaves. The moonlight seemed to illuminate the trail leading toward the scream. Rachael didn't think that could be a coincidence.

The pair ran into a clearing. The same thick, craggily trees rimmed the edges, but there was nothing in the middle of the forest here save a crumpled body and forest debris. The moon illuminated her blonde hair as she lay face down in the leaves.

She was breathing. Rachael could see that even from her spot on the edge of the clearing. Graham only hesitated for a second to observe the situation, clearly looking for enemies hiding in the shadows. Rachael didn't see anyone lurking there, waiting for the couple to step out into the open so that she could pounce, but when Graham started toward Chell, Rachael didn't move. She kept her eyes open and her hands ready.

Graham kneeled down next to the fallen woman. "Chell?" he said, the concern in his voice creating a waiver in his generally confident tenor. "What happened?"

She struggled to sit up, her hands slipping on the grass. Even from a distance, Rachael could see that it was because she was sitting in a pool of blood. Whether it was hers or someone else's she couldn't say, until Graham helped lift the girl to sitting and Rachael got a good look at her throat.

It was slit, nearly from ear to ear. Crimson streaks lined her neck, dripping down to the white T-shirt she wore beneath her black leather jacket, the collar almost black with the sticky substance.

Graham whispered a curse word and rested her head against his bicep. "Chell, God, I'm so sorry."

"Gr--raham…" she stuttered. She was lifting her hand slightly and gesturing toward the forest behind where he was sitting, an indication he wasn't the Graham she was currently concerned with.

"We'll get to him," the human version of her boyfriend assured her. "It'll be okay."

Rachael didn't think that would be the case, considering it was clear this Chell was about to expire, but she couldn't blame him for trying to comfort her. Tears were streaming down his cheeks, his chest heaving, and Rachael realized he was reliving that night when he'd lost his own Chell.

She needed to do something.

But what? Even though she had immense powers, the kind that could shift worlds and cause histories to change and collide, she'd never even attempted to save a human before, let alone a vampire.

She could try, though. As Chell's chest began to still, her breaths becoming more shallow, Rachael summoned the energy around her, pulling it into her hands, the way her father had taught her to. He'd been showing her how to use it to distort nature and open a portal, but was it possible she could use the same energy for other purposes?

Once she had what she hoped was an ample supply of light in her hands, Rachael studied it, softened it, imagined it was a healing light. In her mind's eye, she saw the light glowing around Chell's neck, pulling the broken, mangled skin back together, healing the vessels and veins, knitting the muscles and skeleton back together.

Without any more time to spare, Rachael sent the light over to Chell. The glow surrounded the wound, continuing to brighten the darkness of the forest.

"What are you doing?" Graham asked, his voice more curious than accusatory. Chell began to make small gasping sounds, as if she were struggling to breathe but couldn't. The gurgling noise she'd been making before faded away all together, and her body began to vibrate slightly as the light seeped into her throat.

Graham kept a grip on her as Chell's vibrations became more violent. "Rachael--I'm not sure this is working."

"Well, it couldn't make it worse," she reminded him. If she had done nothing, the vampire likely would've breathed her last by now. The light continued to soak into her throat, where Rachael had directed it, but it was also spreading. Rachael watched in wonder as it seeped up her chin and down toward her chest.

His eyes wide, Graham asked, "What's happening?"

"I don't know," Rachael admitted, watching the light continue to move across Chell's body, picking up speed as it ebbed and flowed to the top of her head and down toward her thighs and lower. She wasn't making that awful noise anymore, and though the glow around the slice in her neck was brighter than the rest of her body, it seemed as if the wound was healing. No more blood flowed from the gash; the skin appeared to be weaving itself back together.

So what was the rest of the light doing?

Rachael continued to watch the light engulf Chell, though it didn't touch Graham. Once she was completely bathed in the soft glow, the light pulsated around her for several moments before it began to fade, the air around them reabsorbing the energy it had donated to Rachael when she'd needed it.

Chell's body slumped back against Graham, her eyes closed, her chest barely rising and falling with each shallow breath. The blood still covered her shirt, but it was clear now that her neck was no longer gaping open. Rachael had managed to close that up. Hopefully, everything was healed on the inside, too, so that when Chell opened her eyes, she'd be back to the way she was before the unfortunate encounter with whatever the hell had tried to take her out.

Over the radio, Rachael heard Jared's voice, his tone urgent. As she was doing her best to put Chell back together, she'd heard several calls from her teammates checking in, as Graham had instructed them to, but she'd been able to ignore them. This wasn't quite as easy to tune out. Jared was shouting that he'd found Vampire Rachael and Vampire Graham. He needed back-up.

Graham didn't seem to hear the request, though. He was too busy staring at Chell's beautiful face, illuminated by the moonlight.

"Graham?" Rachael said. "We need to go help Jared."

"Huh?" he asked, blinking a few times as he looked up at her.

"Jared's calling for backup. We need to go."

"But... we can't just leave her here. What if whatever did this to her comes back?"

"I think whatever did it to her was Vampire Rachael, and that's what Jared needs help with. She'll be fine for a few minutes. Come on."

She took a few steps toward him, her hand extended, and could easily see the uncertainty in his eyes as he oscillated between continuing to sit in the middle of the clearing, holding the doppelgängers of his dead fiancée, or taking the hand of his current girlfriend and heading out to find the demon who'd done this to her.

Shaking his head, as if he'd just come back to himself, Graham gently moved Chell so that he could work his way out from underneath her, lying her back onto the grass with care. Rachael tried not to let it bother her. Chell might live, but she'd still be a vampire, and she was still with a different version of the man she loved, so there was really no reason to be jealous. Still, she didn't like seeing him so fixated on someone who looked exactly like the woman he'd lost.

Graham didn't take her hand. He didn't even turn to look at her. Instead, he started a conversation with Jared and then rushed off in the opposite direction, leaving Rachael to step over Chell and follow him. Chills went up her spine as she took off into the dark forest, and they had nothing to do with the vampire she was running toward.

ONLY ONE THING TO DO

Rachael

CHASING GRAHAM through the woods toward the standoff between the rest of their team and a vampire version of herself had Rachael's pulse pounding. Graham was running at full speed, despite the uneven, unfamiliar terrain. He seemed to be having no difficulty, but Rachael was certain she was about to trip or have her hair ripped out by a low-lying tree branch. He must've recovered from his own injuries by now.

And she didn't want to be running after him under these circumstances anyway. Not after the way he'd interacted with Vampire Chell when Rachael was healing her. The way he'd looked at her, as if the woman who had been dying was his true fiancée and not just some otherworldly version of her, made Rachael's stomach tighten. When he looked at the bloodsucker, was he seeing the woman he'd lost?

Thoughts about the psychological ramifications of seeing the face of a dead loved one on the body of an enemy species would have to wait. In the distance, Rachael saw a glowing between the trees and imagined that was the vampire version of her conjuring the energy around her to defend herself and whomever else she may be in the company of.

She came up behind Graham, who was standing in front of Vampire Rachael, the rest of the team having spread out to make room for their leader. In front of her, Rachael held the vampire version of Graham, his head in a precarious position, as if she were contemplating twisting until it popped off. The glow was present around her hands, but she didn't let go of Vampire Graham to conjure any power. Maybe she didn't have to use her hands the way that Rachael did. She was clearly more skilled in that area.

The bloodsucker was also cornered and panicked. Rachael could read that expression in the familiar eyes staring back at her. The other version of herself was trying desperately to hide how she was feeling, but she couldn't hide it from herself.

Graham was trying to negotiate with her, no doubt a bit uncomfortable seeing a duplicate of himself in such a precarious position. He had his hands out in front of him, his voice low as he tried to negotiate with the desperate woman in front of him. "Come on, Rachael. You know you don't want to hurt him. You love him, don't you?"

Her fangs were bared as she replied, "I do love him, but there are plenty of Grahams in the sea. If I can't have this one, there's always you."

Their leader snarled slightly, pulling his head back as he contemplated what she was saying. He didn't bother to try to explain why that wouldn't happen, though. "Rachael, what is it that you want us to do? Let you go? Do you want to release Graham and then fade away into another world?"

Rachael felt her hands clench into fists at the idea. They had her-- finally. Would Graham seriously consider letting her back away into the forest and disappear before they could end this once and for all? Or was he merely trying to establish the circumstances?

Around her, the team grew restless at the suggestion. Jazz was already shifting her weight back and forth on her feet, anxious to start the fight. Jared had a scowl on his face that told Rachael he was wishing he would've just handled the situation himself, and Sammi was practically coming unglued, she wanted to strike out at the vampire so badly.

"I know that won't happen," Vampire Rachael spat. "The only thing that's keeping you back now is that you know you wouldn't be here if it wasn't for this Graham helping to save your life."

"The only reason you haven't been obliterated is because we have so much respect for our leader." Sammi was glaring at the vampire as if all the hate she'd collected over the months for Rachael the hunter needed to be unleashed on the vampire's ass.

Standing behind Graham, in his shadow, Rachael contemplated what to do. Sammi's words were true. She had no desire to go against what Graham wanted for the team. At the same time, if he was willing to let her go now, when they'd finally chased her down, she wouldn't be happy with that decision. Could she summon the energy now to do enough damage to Vampire Rachael that someone else could swoop in and grab Vampire Graham, pulling him to safety so that the rest of them could attack her?

Would finding out go against orders from Graham, or was he secretly waiting for her to take the initiative and put her powers to use?

There was only one way to find out. As soon as Rachael started to summon the energy around her, she knew that Vampire Rachael would know for sure she was there. Perhaps she knew already. The element of surprise would've been helpful, but she'd have to assume she wouldn't have it.

With a deep breath, Rachael spread her hands apart and called the energy from around her to her hands. Out of the air it came, springing out of the trees, from the ground, down from the heavens. Never had it collected so swiftly. In a matter of seconds, she had enormous balls of blue, glowing light in each hand.

Graham swiveled to see what was happening behind him, and when he realized what she was doing, and how quickly it was happening, he stepped aside. Now, Rachael was standing directly across from the dark version of herself, nothing between them but twenty feet of dancing air--and Vampire Graham who was looking at Rachael out of the corner of his eye, a pleading expression on his handsome face.

"Let him go," she said, her voice even. She was in complete control of this situation, and it seemed the power around her was on her side as well.

Vampire Rachael smirked. "You think you're as powerful as I am? We might be nearly identical in many ways, Rachael, but you do not have the strength or practice that I have."

"I might not have the practice, but I do have the strength. And I have the overwhelming desire to rip your fucking head off and send you to whatever dimension lies on the other side of death."

Drawing her red lips back further so that her fangs were more prominent, Vampire Rachael laughed and then said, "I've already crossed that bridge, Rach. And this is it."

Realizing she was saying she was already undead, so it didn't scare her, Rachael narrowed her eyes. "Well, then let's see what a little destruction feels like."

The balls of light were larger than basketballs now, resting in the palms of her hands, and Rachael knew now was her only chance. She had to hope her aim was good enough not to hurt Vampire Graham, but she couldn't wait anymore. If she were going to end this, now was her chance. With all of the strength she could gather, she sent a direct beam of energy across the chasm, aiming for Vampire Rachael's head. With any luck, it would knock her backward, and she'd have to release Graham.

Before the blast reached her, in a split second, Vampire Rachael swiveled Graham's head--hard. He let out a groan and fell to the ground, landing at her feet. His head was still attached to his body, but his neck might be broken. Rachael didn't have time to check and see. Vampire Rachael countered her surge of energy with one of her own. Ironically, the light thrown from the dark creature was a soft white. It collided with Rachael's beams, the two of them throwing sparks into the sky as they countered each other.

Standing there in the middle of the forest, facing her evil side head-on, Rachael knew she'd have to do what her father taught her and summon more energy without releasing her hands from their position. Was she strong enough to do that? Was there anything the rest of the team could do without stepping between them and inadvertently getting hurt? This had to end--now--no matter what.

Rachael buckled down, drew another deep breath, and with her mind, called on any remaining energy around them to come to her aid. It had to be enough. This had to end, and Vampire Rachael had to be destroyed. Once and for all.

BATTLE TO THE DEATH

Rachael

' balls of light continue to light the sky as Rachael faced off against the vampire version of herself. At the feet of the monster, Vampire Graham moaned, his neck twisted at an odd angle. In the back of her mind, Rachael thought perhaps she could end this standoff quickly enough to come to his aid, the same way she had his girlfriend, Vampire Chell, but Vampire Rachael wasn't going down without a fight, and as the two stood there, both hands in the air, battling one another, it seemed neither of them had the upper hand.

Continuing to pull energy from the world around her, Rachael saw a slight increase in her powers as the vampire took a step backward, surely trying to rally her own power to fight back. She lunged forward then, sending Rachael stumbling. Determination set in, and she gritted her teeth, wondering if the rest of her team would jump in and do something, and if so, how the vampire would react.

It only took a second for her to get her response. Another blue light lit up the forest as Graham sent a beam at Vampire Rachael from her right. She had to shift to counter it, pulling one hand away from Rachael's powers. Not every member of Rachael's team was able to create the sort of power they could shoot across at the enemy the way she and Graham were, but Sammi was, and soon, her beam joined in, too.

Vampire Rachael was overwhelmed. She couldn't shift to counter the third attack, so she was taking a direct hit from Sammi, full force, in her right side and abdomen. The pain was evident on her face as she gritted her teeth and narrowed her eyes. She had to know this was it, the end of her. How could she possibly fight all three of them off? And there were more team members standing nearby who could open fire with their guns to weaken her. Why were they just standing there?

It must've been a lack of directions from Graham or shock, but Jared moved first, raising his gun and unloading several rounds into Vampire Rachael's torso. The others did the same, and to Rachael's ear, it suddenly sounded like one of those gangster movies from the 1930s when the head mobster finally gets his comeuppance.

Vampire Rachael began to bend at the waist, stumbling back, shrinking with every bullet that hit her, but not going down, not yet. Her mouth was moving, though Rachael couldn't understand what she was saying. Calling on the energy around her would do no good, as Rachael was sucking all of that away from her, and there seemed to be no other vampires around to help her.

As she crumpled to her knees, a whooshing sound from between the trees behind her drew Rachael's attention to the blackness around them. It was a noise she couldn't place, and it was loud enough to be heard over the expenditure of bullets flying from several weapons. What was that?

The others heard it, too. Jared even stopped firing to turn and look behind him. If Vampire Rachael was attempting to open another portal to escape, it would have to be the kind that would suck her out of this one, because she wasn't moving, not anymore. Energy still surged from her raised palms, but the rest of her body was on the ground now, next to Vampire Graham, who wasn't moving anymore either.

The sound of air moving rapidly around them increased, and then, another sound met their ears. This was a haunting moan, sort of like the sound a ghost might make on a horror movie right before it moves in to attack. Rachael's eyes bulged as she kept her hands sending the beams of light at Vampire Rachael, but she pulled her attention away from the dying monster to look between the trees.

Then she saw them. What they were exactly, she wasn't sure. She'd never seen anything like them in her entire life. It was as if they were made of gossamer, draped over invisible skeletons that hung in the night sky like Halloween decorations. Except they were moving forward, coming toward the clearing at an alarmingly rapid pace, their bony hands extended. It was difficult to see them because they were a dark gray color, almost the same shade as the night around them. But once Rachael's eyes adjusted, and she could see what was coming, panic welled up inside of her.

What the hell were these things, and how did they defeat them? The screams grew louder as they entered the clearing, and the rest of her team turned to give their attention to the new threat, only Rachael and Graham keeping their focus on Vampire Rachael.

Bullets seemed to do nothing against them as they went right through their gossamer skins. Sammi tried shooting one of them with a concentrated beam of energy from her hands, and the creature screeched, flames catching along what Rachael could only describe as a ragged wing. That seemed to do something, so she quickly aimed for another, and another, but even when they were aflame, they continued to fly, and more were coming.

"This has to end now!" Graham shouted, and Rachael realized he was talking to her. Maybe if Vampire Rachael didn't exist, these monsters would fade away, too. She was still on the ground, though the rest of the team pulling away seemed to have given her a bit of strength back. She was looking up at them now, a defiant scowl on her face, her eyes narrowed.

The vampire couldn't be that much stronger than her, Rachael thought. She refocused on her main enemy, hoping if any of the winged creatures came her way, her team would be able to fight them off. She ducked her head down and moved forward, the sound of approaching wings blocked out by the more important task at hand.

As she stepped closer, she tried to summon more energy from the forest, but there was none to be had. Either she'd used it all up, or these creatures were preventing it from coming to her. She'd have to find another way to defeat Vampire Rachael before she ran out of energy altogether.

Just then, a sharp pain in her shoulder had her reeling around. One of the ragged edges of the gossamer creatures clipped her shoulder. They may look like flimsy fabric, but they were sharp. This close, she could see its eyes, dark glowing orbs in the center of gray nothingness. It shrieked and came at her again.

Reflexively, Rachael turned and shot at it with her powers. It did more than catch on fire. It exploded into a million pieces, sending jagged, sharp scraps of itself everywhere. Rachael had to cover her face for a moment as they rained down on her, which meant she'd completely taken her attention off Vampire Rachael. The shrapnel cut into the bare skin of her hands and neck, unable to penetrate her leather jacket. The sting of a thousand wasps infiltrated her body, but she didn't have time to give into the pain now.

Once she was sure the aftermath of the creature exploding was over, she returned her attention to Vampire Rachel. She'd recovered quickly and was already back on her knees, despite Graham still fighting her. Rachael watched as the monster, bleeding from more gunshots than she could count, increased the power in her left hand and sent it at Graham.

He went flying backward, colliding with a tree, and falling to the ground. Yes, Vampire Rachael was summoning strength from somewhere. But where?

Another creature exploded on the other side of the clearing. Who had done it and how, she didn't know, but the shrieks of pain from the enemy were followed by screams of her teammates as they were covered by the sharp remnants.

And Vampire Rachael began to stand up.

"That's it!" Rachael screamed. "When we kill one of the creatures, she takes their energy! Stop killing them so I can kill her!"

"But… they're cutting us to shreds!" Sammi shouted back.

A quick glimpse in the trainer's direction told Rachael she wasn't exaggerating. Blood was pouring down her face from wounds in her cheeks and the top of her head, not to mention her hands. The rest of the team was in similar straights.

"They can't penetrate leather!" she shouted back. "See if you can protect yourself with that until I get a chance to kill Vampire Rachael."

Maniacal laughter had her head spinning back to the monster across from her who was standing now as confidently as she had been before the onslaught of attacks from the team. "You can't defeat me, Rachael. You're not strong enough. You're not smart enough. You're not enough, Rachael." With that, she sent a blast of power across the darkness, knocking Rachael several steps backward.

But she didn't fall. And she didn't listen to the words of her enemy, either. She didn't need anyone else to tell her she wasn't enough. She'd been telling herself the same things her entire life. And Vampire Rachael knew that. With new resolve, she regained her footing and pressed forward. This was ending today. Right now. And when the smoke cleared, Rachael would prove that she was strong enough. She was smart enough. She was enough.

NO POWER OVER ME

Rachael

With Vampire Rachael's insults fresh in her mind, Rachael dug deep inside of herself and summoned every ounce of energy and power she had left, sending it soaring from her open palms across the expanse to where the bloodsucker stood, bleeding from several gunshot wounds, snarling at her.

As she had last time, Vampire Rachael raised her hands to counter the blow. For a moment, the two beams collided, as they had earlier. But then, Rachael saw hers overpowering the vampire's. She continued to concentrate everything she had inside of her on knocking the woman back to the ground. Even when one of the strange dark creatures began to harass her, sharp teeth she hadn't realized they even had sinking into her ear, Rachael ignored it and concentrated on the vampire to blame for all of this.

Vampire Rachael staggered backward a few steps, her powers faltering, sputtering, sparking, dying. Rachael took advantage, stepping forward, closing the gap between them. She was ending this right now, even if that damn beast chewed her ear off in the process.

A blast from somewhere to her left hit the gossamer creature, causing it to shriek and pull back. She assumed it had come from one of her teammates. A quick turn of her head revealed Sammi with a satisfied nod. The creature was in pain but not dead. Vampire Rachael could only draw their power if they actually died, not when they were merely injured. It fell back, leaving Rachael to move forward unhindered.

"You can't... kill me...." Vampire Rachael was lying on the ground now, flat on her back as the light continued to weaken her body, causing her to shudder and shake. "We're the same!"

"We are not the same!" Rachael looked down at her, unable to believe someone who looked so much like her could be so evil. "I don't know what happened to you to make you like this, but you and I are not the same. And your evil reign ends today."

The vampire's eyeballs were rolling into the back of her head, drool coming from the side of her mouth. Rachael pulled a silver blade from its sheath and dropped to one knee, keeping the other palm open so that her powers continued to flow.

A quick jab to the jugular, and Vampire Rachael sputtered a few times, but she didn't scream. Rachael needed both hands now, but she was fairly certain her counterpart was done. Grabbing ahold of hair that felt exactly the same as hers, she began to saw. Blood spurted up at her, coating the trunk of a nearby tree, and creating a red river beneath the body of her enemy. Rachael continued to slice her knife through the flesh and sinews, the same sticky substance dripping from Vampire Rachael's mouth and nose. With one last hack of her knife, she finished the job, severing Vampire Rachael's head. She left it lying next to the body and stood back up. Her hand was covered with the crimson substance and she had a stain on the knee of her pants. But it was over. She was dead--at last.

Wiping sweat from her forehead with the back of her clean hand, Rachael took a deep breath and shoved her knife back into its sheath. The creatures hadn't disappeared when Vampire Rachael died. Grunting from exhaustion, Rachael said, "Okay--you can blow 'em up now. Just remember they rain down on you like a million tiny pieces of glass."

Her teammates didn't need to be told twice. The ones that could immediately started exploding the creatures. Rachael helped out as well, aiming for the wounded creature who had been nibbling on her ear first, sending it shattering across the forest. She didn't even want to know how badly her ear was injured. Now that she was done with Vampire Rachael, it was stinging horribly.

She blew a few more creatures out of the sky and then glanced down to see her Graham kneeling over Vampire Graham, checking for a pulse. "Is he still alive?" she asked. She'd just assumed, with the odd angle his neck was bent at, he'd have to be dead.

When Graham looked up at her, she saw the answer in his expression before he even slowly shook his head. It was too bad. Vampire Graham had helped them. He was a good guy, and Rachael had been hopeful that he and his Vampire Chell could return to the world from which they came and live a happy life together, now that Vampire Rachael was no longer around to torment her.

Once all of the gray creatures were gone, the forest became relatively silent again, only the sounds of the odd birds and other animals calling to one another and the hum of insects met their ears as they stood assessing the situation.

"I guess it's all over now," Jazz said, breaking the silence. "You did good, Rach."

"Thank you," Rachael said, still absently wiping at the blood on her hand. "You all helped a lot. I couldn't have done it without you."

"I don't know. That power of yours is pretty spectacular," Sammi added. It wasn't like her to compliment Rachael, so the words immediately brought a smile to her face.

"Can we go home now?" Marcy asked, looking as exhausted as Rachael felt. "I think I could sleep for seven or eight days."

"Not yet." Graham was up from where he'd been kneeling next to the vampire version of himself. "We need to get Chell."

"Vampire Chell," Rachael corrected.

"Right."

That uneasy feeling from earlier settled in the pit of her stomach. Had her boyfriend completely forgotten that the woman they'd saved earlier was a vampire and not his dead fiancée?

"Where is she?" Sammi asked. "Is she okay?"

"She was in pretty bad shape when we came across her, but Rachael fixed her," he replied, walking slowly in the direction where they'd left the woman lying.

"Fixed her? How?" Jared's eyes were wide as he contemplated the question.

"I don't know," Rachael admitted. "But I did. Maybe those powers only work on their kind or something."

"Or maybe there's more to Rachael than we realize," Flint noted, a look of admiration on his face.

Not knowing what to say to that, Rachael felt her face turn pink as she looked away. She doubted that. Could she heal her fellow hunters? Everyone had cuts and scrapes from those creatures. It would be a good time to try.

Before she got the opportunity, the sound of footsteps coming from between the trees alerted them that someone was approaching. Rachael took a deep breath. She wasn't sure any of them could handle another round of attacks now, but Vampire Rachael had been working with some pretty nasty vampires, and none of them had been seen or heard from since Rachael and her friends stepped foot in this reality--unless that's who was coming through the trees.

A silhouette appeared, and Rachael readied herself for another fight. She was tired, but she wasn't going down now, not after what she'd just done. If she could kill Vampire Rachael, she could kill anyone, including whoever was coming for them next.

WHAT ARE THOSE CREATURES?

Rachael

THE TEAM STOOD STILL, staring at the figure emerging from the shadows, weapons at the ready, in case they were needed again, but as the lone figure stepped into the clearing, it became evident none of that was necessary.

It was Vampire Chell. The fact that she was up and walking after the way Rachael and Graham had left her not long ago was remarkable. She looked completely healed, as if nothing had ever happened to her. The only telltale sign was the blood on her clothing. Her face wasn't even pale.

She took a few hesitant steps, not sure what to do with so many hunters watching her so closely. It wasn't until Graham moved toward her that everyone relaxed. He rushed to her side. "Chell, are you okay?"

It made sense to Rachael that he wouldn't call her Vampire Chell to her face, but it still stung. Did he really think she was just plain Chell? The girl he'd been engaged to marry?

She let him put his arms around her as if he was her Graham.

Rachael couldn't help but look at the body on the ground. Chell would see him soon enough. Then, it was no doubt her Graham would be there to comfort the bloodsucker.

"I'm okay," she said, her voice not quite as strong as normal. "I'm a little woozy. Where's Graham--my Graham?"

Graham the hunter let out a sigh and slid his hands down to her elbows, looking her in the eyes. "We're so sorry, Chell. We did everything we could to try to save him, but in the end, Vampire Rachael ended him."

Chell made a little gasping sound before tears began to cascade down her cheeks. Graham pulled her close, holding her head against his shoulder. Rachael had to look away. She turned around and took a few steps, trying to shut out the sobs of the brokenhearted vampire.

The rest of the team was standing around, awkwardly debating what to do, but then Rachael felt a hand on her shoulder and knew without turning around that it was Jared. If anyone knew how she felt at the moment, it was him, and it was kind of him to attempt to comfort her despite everything Rachael had put him through.

After a few moments, Chell's voice hit her ear. "Can I see him?"

"Of course," Graham replied. Rachael turned around then, and watched as her boyfriend led a woman who looked exactly like his ex-fiancée over to a dead version of himself. It was all too surreal.

Chell kneeled down next to her lost love, the tears coming harder now as she lamented her loss. She laid her head on his chest for a few moments, all the while, Graham rubbing her back, whispering his condolences. He certainly knew what it was like to lose someone he loved so tragically.

"I wish… I wish I would've gotten a chance to say goodbye," Chell said, attempting to dry up her tears.

"He knew how much you loved him," Graham assured her, and it was reassuring coming from him, since he would've known exactly how Vampire Graham felt about his fiancée.

The rest of the team came together, stepping closer to where Rachael and Jared were watching the scene, the professor's hand still on her shoulder. "What will you do now?" Sammi asked Chell. "Do you want us to help you take him back to your reality?"

"No, I don't think he'd like that. We never really fit in there. So many of the other vampires were hostile, always wanting to kill just for the sake of killing. I think we should just bury him here, if that's possible."

"Maybe we could go back and get a shovel or something…." Flint glanced around as if he might see one sitting by a tree.

Rachael knew her powers had begun to strengthen again. "I think I might be able to do it," she volunteered. Helping Chell in this instance just seemed like the right thing to do, even if she was unbelievably jealous of the pull she had on Graham.

Closing her eyes in concentration, Rachael worked on pulling power from around her and asked the forest floor to open and receive Graham, making him part of the wondrous natural beauty. When she opened her eyes, the ground next to where Graham lay had begun to move, the grass and dirt lifting into the sky above their heads, mostly in one piece, though some debris sprinkled down around them.

Flint and Graham moved to lift the body and carefully set it in the hole. It wasn't quite six feet, but it would do, and Rachael hadn't been specific with her request. Once he was in, Chell kissed her hand and blew him a kiss, and then Rachael asked the forest to fall back into place.

The floating mound of earth slowly descended, resuming its original location. It looked as if it had never been displaced to begin with. Chell lay down on top of the grass and began to cry again. Graham put his arm around her shoulders, but he wasn't saying anything this time, only silently comforting her.

"What about Vampire Rachael?" Jazz asked. "Should we bury her?"

"Why? She deserves to be eaten by wild animals." Sammi seemed to have shifted some of her hate from her fellow hunter Rachael to the monster.

"I wonder what kind of wild animals live here," Jazz wondered aloud, her eyes tracing the trees as she glanced around.

As if in response, an odd howling noise that didn't quite sound like a wolf or a coyote echoed in the distance.

"I'd rather not find out," Marcy admitted. "Perhaps we should find a way out of here."

"Oh, I'll get you out of here, just as soon as Graham and Vam--uh--Chell are ready to go," Jazz assured them. She'd almost said Vampire Chell, which made Rachael smile, but she hid it by looking away.

"We still don't know what Chell's going to do," Sammi reminded them. "She can't come back to our world and expect to stay there as a vampire. We have rules against that."

"I can take her somewhere else," Jazz volunteered.

"That would be scary. To just be dumped into another realm not knowing anyone or anything." Flint shook his head as he spoke.

"Tell me about it," Rachael muttered. She thought perhaps Chell would be more inclined to leave if Graham had a proper grave marker, so she found two sticks on the ground and fashioned them into a cross, using her powers to fuse them. It might be ironic to mark the grave of a vampire with a cross, but it would have to do. She stuck it into the ground, causing both Chell and Graham to look up at her. "We need to go," she said quietly.

Chell sat back on her heels, wiping at her eyes and nose again. "I'm sorry. I didn't mean to make you wait."

"No, it's okay. It's just… there's an odd howling out there, and we'd just as soon get home. It's been a long… year." Anything less than that would be untrue. "What are you planning to do, Chell?"

"Well, I don't know…." She looked at Graham and then at the other team members. "I can't go home. Not like this."

"You mean alone?" Graham asked, his hand still resting on her shoulder.

The blonde shook her head. "No, as hard as that would be, I would consider it. It's just… I can't go back to my realm in my current state."

The team exchanged puzzled glances. "What do you mean?" Jazz asked for all of them.

"I mean…when Rachael did whatever she did to save me, she changed me. I'm not what I was before."

For the first time since the woman had appeared from between the trees, Rachael realized it was more than just her wounds that had been fixed. There were other differences about her too. She wasn't pale anymore. Her eyes were their normal color, not a goldish brown, and her fangs were gone.

"You're not a vampire anymore?" Rachael asked.

Chell shook her head. "No. I'm not. Thank you, Rachael."

Rachael didn't know what to say. She'd had no idea she had the power to turn a vampire back into a human. The look on Graham's face was enough to make her wish she had never done it. He was beaming with joy as he stared at the woman next to him. Rachael swallowed hard, her heart breaking and replied, "You're welcome."

QUIET TIME

Rachael

THE NIGHT SOUNDS outside of the Academy were not the same as the forests they'd visited recently, but there was still quite a bit of chatter amongst the insects and the birds. Rachael sat on a bench beneath a tree, the dorm building behind her, staring out at the gardens, her mind completely blank.

At least, she wished it was. As much as she tried to keep her mind off what was happening in the building behind her, it was difficult to do so. They'd been back from the hunt for about an hour now. Everyone else had rushed in to shower and get some sleep. She'd perched herself here, trying to make peace with what was happening between Graham and Chell. He'd explained on the ride home that he felt like he needed to help her get settled, and she'd nodded, but she still didn't want to accept that her boyfriend was falling back in love with a woman who looked like his fiancée who'd passed away. It was a lot to get her mind around.

She knew he didn't want to hurt her, and as far as she could tell, he might not even be aware of what was happening. But she could see it as clear as the light of day. It wouldn't be long until he came to her and said he wanted to give things a chance with this Chell. Even though he knew it wasn't his Chell, she was so much the same, he'd feel compelled to give it a try. What could Rachael do but nod and smile and say she understood, even if it broke her heart, even if she didn't really understand, even if she wished she hadn't ever made Chell a human to begin with.

A solitary tear slipped from her eye as she thought back through all of the good times she'd had with Graham. When she was writing about him, she'd done her best to make him the perfect guy, and in so many ways, he'd lived up to her expectations. He was dashingly handsome, built like a Greek god, polite, kind, thoughtful, intelligent, a bold leader--everything a girl could want in a guy. They'd had plenty of adventures together, and she hoped they could remain friends, even though it was evident their run as lovers was over.

A sound behind her had her head whipping around as if she was out on a hunt, and it might be a vampire sneaking up on her. It wasn't--but it was almost as bad. Sammi was approaching her, the expression on her face unreadable. The woman had hated her for so long, Rachael assumed she wouldn't have anything good to say about the accidental return of her sister--who wasn't her sister.

"Hi, Rach." Her tone was softer than Rachael ever remembered it being before. "Can I have a seat?"

"Sure," Rachael replied. The bench was plenty big enough, and she was curious to hear what Sammi had to say, even if it ended up being insulting and rude. "How are you?"

A small smile graced her face. "Better than I have been in a long time. I got a chance to talk to Chell on the way here. She reminds me a lot of my sister. She said her sister was killed in a vampire attack several years ago, and she just couldn't get over how much I remind her of the sister she lost."

"That's... great." Rachael wasn't sure what she was supposed to say. It was still a struggle to wrap her mind around all of these different versions of everyone.

"Yeah, so... I just wanted to say thank you. I mean, I know it's not the same. She's not my sister, and nothing can ever bring our Chell back. But she's a close second. At least, I think she is. It'll be good to have her around, I think. Graham is helping her get settled in one of the student dorms. I think the plan is to have her join the team, if she wants to, once she gets her bearings."

Rachael nodded. She'd made that assumption already. "He seems to be of the same opinion you are--that she's a close second."

"Yeah." Sammi drew in a deep breath and let it out slowly, her eyes flickering around in contemplation. "About that... I'm really sorry your good deed backfired in your face. That really sucks."

Somehow, Rachael managed a small smile at the wording. "Yeah, it does. But... if she makes him happy, or has the potential to make him happy, that's all that matters. Graham has been through a lot. I still love him, but I know I have to let him go." She shrugged, as if that somehow simplified her decision. "It's just easier for all of us this way, if I don't make a big deal out of it."

"Maybe he'll see that she's not the same, or he'll realize he would rather be with you," Sammi suggested, clearly trying to be optimistic, not her strong point.

"Maybe. But I won't be holding my breath. You know, I don't feel as bad about it as I expected. I thought, if Graham and I ever broke up, I'd be devastated. But I'm not." It was an odd sensation, like she'd somehow realized this was what was going to happen all along.

Sammi's face said she didn't quite believe her, but she said, "That's great."

"Yeah." Rachael nodded along, as if saying it had somehow made it so.

"Well, I think I'll head inside and get some sleep. You coming?"

"No, not yet." Rachael wasn't sure what it was that made her want to continue to sit outside, but she needed a few more moments. It wasn't as if she wasn't exhausted, sore, and had some cuts that needed to be taken care of, thanks to those stupid flying gray monsters, but she wasn't ready to go inside to the bed she'd shared with Graham just yet.

"Probably just as well. Looks like someone else wants to talk to you." Sammi leaned over and patted Rachael on the hand and then left, the kind gesture catching Rachael so off guard that she didn't even catch what Sammi had said until she turned her head to follow Sammi inside and saw him standing there in the shadows, waiting for her to leave.

Rachael caught her breath and a smile slid into place unforced. Maybe that's why she wasn't quite as upset about Graham as she should've been. As he slowly walked her direction, that contemplative look on his face that let her know he was deeply considering every word that was about to come out of his mouth, Rachael turned and gestured for him to have a seat. "Hello, Dr. McCall."

Sitting down about a foot from her, he replied, "I think it's time you started calling me Jared."

HE'S THERE

Rachael

TAKING A DEEP BREATH IN, Rachael studied her former professor, not sure what to say. Of course, she hadn't always called him Dr. McCall. Most of the time, she did call him Jared. Especially back when their relationship was more romantic, before she'd decided she'd rather be with Graham. After that, she'd inadvertently become more formal. She wouldn't have blamed him if he was there to laugh in her face and ask her how it feels, but it was clear by his expression, as he sat there, a contemplative look on his handsome face, trying to decide what to say to her that he wasn't there to give her a hard time. In fact, the way Jared had treated her before they'd left to come home from the other realm and on the way back implied that he actually felt sorry for her. Possibly more.

"How are you doing?" he asked, a sympathy in his eyes. "Are you okay?"

Rachael shrugged. "I guess so. Do I have any choice?" She glanced back at the building, as if she could somehow see through the brick exterior to whatever room Graham and Chell were in now, getting her situated. Of course, she couldn't, so she turned back to face Jared. "It'll be weird for a while, but I'll figure it out."

A half smile pulled at the right side of his face. "Yeah. It gets easier after a while."

She returned the smile. "I'm sorry. You know I never meant to hurt you."

"I know. And I don't think Graham wants to hurt you either. I think... sometimes it's impossible to say no to a tug that strong. The heart knows what it wants, as they say. Eventually, he might change his mind and wish he'd made another choice."

"I'm not going to stand around and wait." Rachael had already decided that she wasn't going to put her entire life on hold to see if Graham ended up regretting his decision. No, if opportunities to date other men came about, she'd weigh them as a single woman, not as someone hopelessly in love with a man she would likely never be able to claim as hers again.

"I'm glad to hear that," Jared said, scooting slightly closer to her. "Because... when you're ready, if you want, I'd really like to see if my decision to wait around was the right one."

Rachael's eyebrows raised. "You've been waiting around--for me?"

It was his turn to shrug like it was no big deal. "I mean... I don't exactly have women banging down my door like... some people. But, yeah. I wished you and Graham the best. I was hoping for your sake the two of you would end up finding your happily ever after. But deep down inside, I guess I always had a feeling it might not work out. And... I wanted to be here for you if you needed a soft place to fall."

Rachael felt tears in her eyes. Everything he said was so unbelievably sweet. The last thing she wanted to do was start crying because she had a feeling, once those floodgates opened, they would never close again. Reaching across the small space between them, she took his hand. "Thanks, Jared. I will probably need a little bit of time to clear my head. But when I'm ready, I'd definitely like to give us another shot. We had a lot of fun together, and I really like you. I do. I just... thought Graham was my dream man. I thought I'd designed him to be the perfect guy for me. It turns out, maybe he's perfect for everyone. Or maybe he's not perfect at all."

Jared scooted even closer to her so that their knees were touching. "Well, when you're ready, you've got my number. In the meantime, if you need anything else, let me know." He wrapped his arms around her, and Rachael put her head on his shoulder, embracing him in a tight hug.

She closed her eyes and breathed him in, remembering how good he'd been to her, how he'd always gone out of his way to put her first, how it had felt that first time he'd kissed her, outside of Frank's house when she was coming undone and needed a jolt back to reality. The scent of his aftershave, a hint of the ocean mingled with the deep woods, had her head spinning again, just like it used to, and when Jared released her, for a moment, she hoped he'd kiss her.

He didn't though, and once there was space between them again, she remembered she hadn't technically broken up with Graham yet. For a brief second, her mind went to a dark place, and she wondered if that had stopped him from kissing Chell. Surely, he'd give the woman some time. Her fiancé had just died after all, and even though it was a different version of the same man, it wasn't exactly the same....

"Are you coming in?" Jared asked, bringing her back to the bench.

"Oh, yeah. In a few minutes."

"Okay. Let me know if you need anything." He patted her knee and stood, smiling down at her for a second before he turned to head inside.

A thought entered her mind as he was walking away. "Jared, do you know what room Chell's moving into?"

"Yeah, 425."

"Thanks."

He stared at her for a second, one eyebrow arched in question, but he didn't ask why she wanted to know, and Rachael didn't explain. Jared turned and headed back to the building.

Rachael took a few deep breaths to still herself. She knew what she needed to do next. It wouldn't be easy, but if she could kill a powerful vampire version of herself, she could do anything, couldn't she?

After a few moments of mental preparation, she stood and headed inside, ready to put this chapter of her life to rest so that she could embark on a new one. Whether that would be with Jared, someone else, or all alone, she didn't know yet, but she was about to find out.

LET HIM GO

Rachael

THE SOUND of her heavy boots echoing off the hallway floor wasn't loud enough to muffle the laughter she heard coming from Chell's new room this time of night when the rest of the dorm rooms were quiet. Rachael narrowed her eyes, particularly when she heard Graham's laughter mingled with Chell's. The woman had just lost her fiancé, for God's sake! Wasn't there any decency left in this world?

Biting back her ugly comments, Rachael knocked on the door, relieved when that brought the laughter to an end. A few seconds later, Chell opened the door, her smile widening when she saw who it was. "Rachael. Hi!"

She couldn't help but check for fangs. There were none. "Hi, Chell. Is Graham still here?" Of course, she knew he was. It wasn't as if she hadn't heard him before she knocked on the door.

"Oh, yeah. Sure. Sorry. I didn't mean to rip him away from you." She opened the door and stepped back into it, and Rachael marveled at her choice of words. Hadn't she, though? Hadn't she?

"It's okay." Rachael still wasn't sure whether or not she meant that, but in light of what she'd come there to say, she'd better get used to it. She stepped inside as he rose from the couch, setting a wine glass on a coaster on the coffee table. Where that had come from in her new apartment, Rachael couldn't say and assumed it wasn't her business.

"Hi," he said, a guilty expression on his face. "We were just... getting Chell situated."

She nodded. She knew what was happening. She'd seen it all over his face since the moment he'd found Chell crumpled up in the forest. Rachael was rethinking her decision to save the woman.... "I know. Can we go somewhere and talk for a few minutes, though?"

"Actually, I really need to get some sleep," Chell said, interlacing her fingers. "Now that I'm a human again... well, I guess I'd better get used to being tired."

"Sure," Graham said, though Rachael couldn't tell if he was agreeing with her request or reinforcing Chell's assessment of her new existence. He stepped over to Chell and patted her on the arm. "I'll see you later. Let me know if you need anything."

She smiled up at him. "Thanks for all of your help."

The grin he gave her reminded Rachael of a high school football player gazing at his cheerleader girlfriend. She shook her head and looked away, absently wondering if Chell had a cell phone so she could call him if she truly did need something.

Graham walked out the door, and Chell wished them both a goodnight before she closed it. Rachael wasn't sure where to begin, but she knew the hallway was no place to have this conversation. Her place was closer. "My room?"

"Sure," he said again, gesturing with his arm for her to lead the way.

They didn't speak on the way to her room, not a single word. Nor did he reach for her hand, like he normally would do. She didn't loop her arm through his or touch him gently on the arm. She stayed slightly in front of him, being careful not to touch him at all, not even with an accidental arm swing.

Once inside her room, they settled on the couch, and Rachael couldn't help but think a glass or two of wine would hit the spot about now. He'd changed clothes and apparently taken a shower. She wondered when he'd had time for that--but then, she had been sitting on that bench for a long time. She still had dried blood and caked dirt on her leather pants and imagined she looked a mess. It was just as well. Maybe it would make this all a bit easier.

"So… you and Chell seem to be getting along really well," she began, hoping he'd make this easy on her and just confess that he wanted to give this new version of his old flame a try.

"Yeah. She's great," he said with a nod, trying to hide the smile that wanted to light up his face. "I'm sorry I haven't spent much time with you since we got back."

"Or any time," she thought to herself. "No, that's okay. I just… I can see that you're focused on her. I'm sure you never imagined you might have another opportunity to get back with Chell, and even though it's not the same Chell that you lost, I can see why you'd want to spend time with her."

Graham nodded slowly, his hands pressed together between his knees. "I'm sorry, Rachael. I'm not sure what to say."

"You don't have to say anything." She couldn't believe those words were coming out of her mouth considering she'd just been praying he'd take the lead. "If you want to give things a try with her, then, I'll let you."

He looked up at her, one eyebrow cocked over those lavender eyes she loved so much. "Really? You'd do that?"

"Sure. It won't be easy, but… I can't leave you wondering. If she is the same as the woman you lost, then, you'll always wonder what might've been. I don't want to hold you, if you want to go."

A solemn expression took over his face as he reached for her hand. "Rachael, I've had such a great time with you. I hope you know, my feelings for you are true. I do care about you, so much. The last thing I'd ever want to do is to hurt you."

"I know that, Graham." She fought back the tears that threatened to fall, knowing if she started crying now, she'd never stop. "I just want you to be happy, and if Chell can do that for you, then that's great. I'll… be okay."

He reached over and pulled her to him, crushing her against his chest, his arms wrapped tightly around her. "God, Rachael. I didn't see any of this coming."

"Me neither." She certainly had no idea she was capable of turning a vampire back into a human. If she'd known she had that power, she would've thought twice about using it. But now, what was done was done.

Graham continued to hold her for a long while, and then, slowly pushed back. "Thank you, Rachael. For everything." He wiped at tears in his eyes, and Rachael felt them forming in her own.

"You're welcome, Graham." She stood and walked to the door, as ready for him to move on as she'd ever be.

He followed her, walking slowly. Before he left, he embraced her one more time, and then he was gone.

Rachael thought back to the day she'd met him. Not the day she'd invented the perfect guy in her head, but the day Graham had shown up at her apartment door in Baltimore and opened her eyes to entire worlds of possibilities she'd never fathomed could actually exist. If it hadn't been for him, she'd still be in Baltimore. Whether or not she'd be working as an accountant or a writer, she couldn't say, but she wouldn't be here at Silverwood Academy. She wouldn't know the strength and power she held in the palm of her hands, and she wouldn't know that sometimes the only thing you can do if you truly love someone is set them free to follow their heart.

Exhausted, she headed to the bathroom to take a shower and wash away the residue from the toughest fights she'd ever endured. She may have lost the one for Graham, but at least she'd defeated Vampire Rachael, and if she could do that, she could do anything.

As she stood beneath the warm water, scrubbing the blood and dirt from her skin, she couldn't help but wonder what would come next. Would it be more vampire versions of people she knew? More unheard of threats like the gray monsters? Or creatures she couldn't even imagine? There were too many realms of possibilities to count.

One thing was for sure. Whatever happened next, she'd be a part of the Silverwood team ready to fight it off for many years to come.

EPILOGUE

"And that is how you summon the energy around you and use it for your own purposes!" Dr. Barnes explained, a large ball of blue light floating above her hand, just as the bell rang. The students didn't stir, waiting for her to extinguish the flickering blue flame and let them go.

Rachael closed her hand, the light dissolving as the energy went back into the air. The students continued to stare, some with their mouths agape. "You may go. I will see you on Monday. Have a good-- safe--weekend."

At her words, the students stood, gathering their books, conversations beginning. Rachael crossed back to her desk in the corner of the room, glad to be done with another week of classes, even though she absolutely loved the three classes she was currently teaching. The Academy was full to capacity, and they were considering building more dormitories to hold all of the prospective students coming up in the next few years. Silverwood was more popular than ever, despite vampire attacks being down across the country, and Rachael was proud to have the opportunity to work with such bright, curious students.

"Great class today, Dr. Barnes!" A lanky kid who normally sat near the back stopped by her desk, pausing to shift his books in his arms. "You think I'll be able to do that one day?"

"Thanks, Pete. Sure. We'll keep working on it until you get it." She smiled at him, her own books tucked in her arm, her bag slung over her shoulder.

He gave her a shy grin and then headed out the door behind the rest of his classmates. Rachael smiled at him. She'd once been that awkward newbie who had no idea what she was capable of. It hadn't lasted long for her, but she remembered the feeling.

Once the kids were out of the way, she headed for the door herself. She had a packed weekend ahead of her, filled with vampire hunting and other work related must-dos, but there was some fun scheduled in there as well.

"How was your last class?" Dr. McCall met her in the hallway right outside of her door, his attaché case in one hand, the other wrapping itself around her waist. "Did you stun them with your powers?"

Rachael smiled and leaned up for a quick kiss, hoping none of the students were watching too closely. She didn't want to be inappropriate in front of the students. "It was great. They were dazzled and amazed."

"Great." He kept his arm around her as they headed down the hallway. "Ready to go meet Graham and Chell for dinner before we go over the plan for the hunt?"

Rachael glanced up at the clock on the wall, just as they passed the giant painting of Graham's relative, the original Silverwood. "It's a little early for dinner, isn't it?"

Jared shrugged. "Do you have something else in mind?"

She turned to face him, stopping dead in her tracks, a devilish grin taking over her face. "I bet I could think of something."

Jared chuckled, taking her left hand in his. He studied the large diamond on her fourth finger. "I knew I was a very smart man for giving you this ring."

Rachael leaned up to kiss him again before saying, "Yes, yes you are."

Keeping her hand in his, he spun her around right there in the hallway, Rachael's black heels clicking on the marble, and then led her to the back of the building, to the closest exit, hurrying her back to their shared apartment, and Rachael went along with a bright smile on her face.

Life hadn't quite turned out the way she'd expected it to, but she was overwhelmingly happy with her life and didn't regret a single decision. Her reality might not have been exactly what she wanted before, so she created a new one, one that would keep vampires at bay and love ever-present, even when the world tipped on its side and went crazy for a bit. Regardless of the circumstances, Rachael's feet were firmly planted, and she knew that Silverwood Academy was exactly where she belonged.

THANK YOU FOR READING! If you enjoyed this book, please check out my other vampire hunter series, The Clandestine Saga, Blood of the Vampire Hunter, The Chronicles of Cassidy, and A Vampire Hunter's Tale. Book one in each series is free!

ALSO BY ID JOHNSON

Stand Alone Titles

<u>All I Want for Christmas is Pooch</u>

(*sweet contemporary romance*)

<u>Christmas Memory</u>

(*sweet contemporary romance*)

<u>Meet Cute Me Under the Mistletoe</u>

(*sweet contemporary romance*)

<u>The Doll Maker's Daughter at Christmas</u>

(*clean romance/historical*)

<u>Pretty Little Monster</u>

(*young adult/suspense*)

<u>The Journey to Normal: Our Family's Life with Autism</u> (*nonfiction*)

<u>Found by the Alpha (fantasy romance)</u>

Love Throughout Time

(*time travel romance*)

Back to Titanic

Back to Gettysburg

Back to Bunker Hill

Back to the Highlands

Back to Port Royal

Silverwood Academy

(*paranormal romance*)

Vampire Hunter

World Builder

Realm Jumper

Celestial Springs

(psychological thriller/literary fiction/women's fiction)

Beneath the Inconstant Moon

The First Mrs. Edwards

Leaving Ginny

The Motherhood

(dystopian romance)

Rain's Rebellion

Rain's Run

Rain's Return

Ashes and Rose Petals

(contemporary romance/retelling of Romeo and Juliet and Cinderella)

Girl in the Attic

Girl From the Tomb

Girl On the Beach

Nashville Country Dreams

(contemporary romance)

Meant to Marry Me

Lead Me Home

You Are the Reason

Forever Love series

(clean romance/historical)

Cordia's Will: A Civil War Story of Love and Loss

Cordia's Hope: A Story of Love on the Frontier

The Clandestine Saga series

(paranormal romance)

Transformation
Resurrection
Repercussion
Absolution
Illumination
Destruction
Annihilation
Obliteration
Termination

A Vampire Hunter's Tale (based on The Clandestine Saga)

(paranormal/alternate history)

Aaron
Jamie
Elliott
Christian

The Chronicles of Cassidy (based on The Clandestine Saga)

(young adult paranormal)

So You Think Your Sister's a Vampire Hunter?
Who Wants to Be a Vampire Hunter?
How Not to Be a Vampire Hunter
My Life As a Teenage Vampire Hunter
Vampire Hunting Isn't for Morons
Vampires Bite and Other Life Lessons
Gone Guardian
Death Does Not Become Her

Blood of the Vampire Hunter (based on The Clandestine Saga)

(paranormal romance)

Night Slayer

Shadow Stalker

Queen Catcher

Mother Hunter

Father Finder

Ghosts of Southampton series

(historical romance)

Prelude

Titanic

Residuum

Lusitania

Heartwarming Holidays Sweet Romance series

(Christian/clean romance)

Melody's Christmas

Christmas Cocoa

Winter Woods

Waiting On Love

Shamrock Hearts

A Blossoming Spring Romance

Firecracker!

Falling in Love

Thankful for You

Melody's Christmas Wedding

The New Year's Date

Charles Town Brides (based on Heartwarming Holidays Sweet Romance)

(Christian/clean romance)

From This Moment

Can't Help Falling in Love

It's Your Love

When You Say Nothing At All

My Girl

Unchained Melody

I Only Have Eyes For You

At Last

The Very Thought of You

Reaper's Hollow

(paranormal/urban fantasy)

Ruin's Lot

Ruin's Promise

Ruin's Legacy

When Kings Collide

(steamy historical romance)

Princess of Silence

Princess of Hearts

Collections

Ghosts of Southampton Books 0-2

Reaper's Hollow Books 1-3

The Clandestine Saga Books 1-3

The Chronicles of Cassidy Books 1-4

Celestial Springs Collection

Heartwarming Holidays Sweet Romance Books 1-3

Heartwarming Holidays Sweet Romance Books 4-7

Websites: https://books2read.com/ap/xX7ZD8/ID-Johnson

For updates, visit www.authoridjohnson.blogspot.com

Follow on Twitter @authoridjohnson

Find me on Facebook at www.facebook.com/IDJohnsonAuthor

Instagram: @authoridjohnson

Follow me on Bookbub: https://www.bookbub.com/authors/id-johnson